HOOPS

A HOOPS NOVELLA

HOLIDAY

KENNEDY RYAN

Proofreading:
Kara Hildebrand

Cover Design:
Letitia Hasser, RBA Designs

Cover Photo: Perrywinkle Photography

Reach Kennedy
kennedyryanwrites.com

ISBN-13: 978-1-7321443-2-3

THE HOOPS SERIES
(3 Interconnected *Standalone* Stories)
FREE In KU!

LONG SHOT (A HOOPS Novel)
Available in Ebook, Audio & Paperback

BLOCK SHOT (A HOOPS Novel)
Banner & Jared's Story
Enemies-to-Lovers | Friends-to-Lovers | Second Chance
⋆Audio coming Jan 31, 2019

Coming March 2019
HOOK SHOT (A HOOPS Novel)
Lotus & Kenan's Story

Be alerted as SOON as it's LIVE:
Text KennedyRyan to 797979

FULL-COURT
PRESS

ONE

Decker

I'M DRIPPING WET AND ALMOST NAKED THE FIRST TIME I MEET AVERY Hughes.

It's my second season in the NBA, and I'm used to conducting interviews at my locker wearing only a towel, with a ring of microphones, recorders, and demanding reporters crowded around me. But *this* reporter, *this* night, from the first look, blindsides me.

We played a shit game.

Correction. For forty-five minutes of regulation, we played a stellar game. That last three minutes—that was some shit, and as the idiot who turned the ball over repeatedly in the closing plays, most of that shit rests squarely on my shoulders.

Post-game and post-shower, I lean against my locker, eyes stuck to the floor while I duck and dodge the flurry of questions flying around my head. I should have taken the fine for not making myself available to the press. That would have cost me less. This costs my pride and the dregs of my patience.

"Can you walk us through that fourth quarter implosion, Deck?" a husky voice raises above the fray tightly encircling me. "Those last few minutes of the game were pretty brutal."

My brows snap together at the rudeness, the audacity of this reporter. Sure, I've fielded tougher questions, but after this kind of game, a win that slipped through our fingers, and me responsible, I'm too raw and not in the mood for it.

"What kind of question . . ."

The half-formed demand withers on my lips when I meet the eyes behind the recorder thrust at me. They are the softest thing about her face. Her chin draws to a point, and her cheekbones flare out like a cat's, rounding into sharp feline femininity. She looks down her keen little nose at me with a touch of disdain and condescension. Her lips are set in a flat, determined line, but that doesn't make them less lush, less kissable. But still . . . the eyes are the softest thing in that face, darkest sable, surrounded by a fan of long, minky lashes. Those eyes lock with mine while she waits. They never lower to scrape over the bare brawn of my shoulders and chest. Don't dip to my waist or the barely knotted towel hanging onto my hip. And definitely don't slide over my legs, still dripping from my shower. Nope, she looks me right in *and only in* my eyes while she waits.

"Well, um . . ." I search for her name on the laminated media credential lanyard resting between a set of perky breasts. "*Avery*, we made some mistakes there at the end."

She tilts her head and lifts her brows to the angle of "obviously" before scooting her mic an inch closer. Her scent, something fresh and wild, like the dark, textured curls rioting around her face, is a high note piercing through all the testosterone rife in the locker room.

"Great night overall. Bad few minutes," I finally answer, crooking my mouth into a smile possible now that I've seen her. "Happens to the best of us on any given night."

I shrug, watching her eyes finally drop to the flexing movement, before snapping back to my face.

Ahhh, made you look, pretty lady.

The dark eyes narrow and those kissable lips part like she already has the next question cocked and loaded, but another reporter butts in with something else. I answer a few more questions, getting impatient to dress and talk to Avery without the watchful eye of every major network. When our media rep shuts down the post-game press, reporters start filing out of the locker room. I consider letting it go. Letting *her* go. I've seen prettier girls, right? I can fuck a different chick in a different city every night. Matter of fact, it's practically my civic duty on behalf of all my brethren who will never have the NBA all-access ass pass. Real talk, I'm already over that. Gorgeous, grasping and vapid. That pretty much describes every woman hanging out in the tunnel after a game. This girl—one look and one question tells me I can't have my way with her. I never could resist a challenge, and when Avery turns to leave, giving me an uninterrupted view of a firm, round ass outlined in her tailored slacks, I know I won't resist her either.

"Avery," I call, holding onto my slipping towel with one hand and gently grabbing her elbow with the other. "Hold up a sec."

She looks pointedly at my hand, so large against her slim arm, like it offends her, before looking back to my face. Some half naked, wet jock a foot taller and grabbing her probably isn't making the best first impression.

"Sorry about that." I drop her arm and flick my head toward my locker. "Could I talk to you for a minute?"

Reluctant curiosity settles on her face, and she takes the few steps back to my corner in the chaos of the locker room.

"I wanted to ask you—" I cut off my words when she thrusts her recorder in the space just above my mouth and below my nose. I push it away with a finger. "Uh . . . off the record."

She lowers the recorder to her side, suppressing what I strongly suspect is a smirk.

"You want to tell me the real reason behind your collapse to-night?" The dark brows take flight over curious eyes and she leans one silk-clad shoulder into the locker door.

"No, I mean . . . I could, yeah. Maybe over a drink or dinner. Our flight doesn't leave until the morning."

Horrified realization unfurls on her face.

"Are you asking me out?" Her incredulous words ring through the room, and I look around a little self-consciously. It just isn't done, approaching a reporter like this. In my defense, most reporters don't have an ass like Avery's.

"Yeah, for a drink or something," I whisper, modeling the appropriate and discrete tone for this kind of conversation, hoping she'll catch on. She seems like a bright girl, after all.

"Or something?" A full-blown frown materializes on her face. "I don't do 'or something' with basketball players. I don't do anything with athletes on my beat."

"I'm on your beat?" I lean into the locker door, too, crossing my arms over my chest. "I haven't seen you before."

"Well you'll be seeing me from now on because I was just assigned." Her gaze drops to my chest and I make my pectoral muscles jump. She rolls her eyes. "And I won't compromise my professional objectivity with the 'or something' you probably have in mind."

"One drink," I urge, shifting against the door.

"My answer is still—" Her gasp chokes out the rest of her sentence when the precariously knotted towel slides right down my hip and plops at my feet. The sight of my dick, slightly erect and on the loose for all the world to see, leaches the air from the room for just a moment, the total quiet before a storm of laughter and good-natured cat calls.

"Oh, shit." Ignoring my teammates' snickers, I scramble to grab the towel from the floor, jerking it back around my waist to cover up my junk. I've been sharing showers and locker rooms since my dick was half this size, so I'm unfazed. Avery, though, looks like she swallowed her little recorder and it's about to come back up with her dinner. Over the wolf whistles, a leftover reporter adds his misplaced mockery to the mix.

"Getting an *exclusive*, are you, Hughes, your first night on the job?" he asks with a leer. "An exposé? Deck would give me the scoop, too, if I had an ass like yours."

What the hell? I'd heard comments like that all my life. Hell, maybe I've even thought them myself. This sport, this industry, is male-dominated, and we're basically overpaid, overgrown adolescents, most of us, until we've been around for a while. Some of us longer than others. Hearing that shit with her standing right here, though, seeing the hurt and irritation spark in her eyes before she quells it, makes me want to knock the bitch-ass reporter's glasses off his face. Laughter from a few others at his rude comment overtakes any hope I have of convincing her. I glare at the idiot already on his way out the door.

"Thanks a lot, asshole," she mutters, jerkily adjusting the bag on her shoulder.

"Yeah," I agree, shaking my head. "He's a piece of work."

"I meant *you*," she says, exasperation evident in her tone. "You're the asshole."

"Me?" I thrust my thumb into my naked chest. "What'd I do?"

"Could you just . . ." she sputters, and gestures in the general area of my groin. "Hold onto your little towel? Those are my colleagues. Do you have any idea how hard it is for a woman in this field? To earn their respect as an equal?"

My mouth opens to commiserate, but I never get the chance.

"The answer is no," she barrels over my would-be response. "You have no idea because you've been catered to and coddled since you made your first triple-double in high school. Those other reporters don't have to worry about being pinched or grabbed on the sly. It doesn't bother them conducting interviews with half-naked men, which I don't mind either until one of them pulls me into a corner and asks for a drink *'or something.'*"

I let those words sink into the quiet that collects around us after her diatribe. By any reasonable measure, this would be considered a rough start, but I've never met a woman who could resist my charm, my smile, my good humor. My tanned half-naked body. If I'm a betting man, I don't think Avery can either.

5

"Soooooo . . . you've been following me since high school?" I break out my fail-proof grin. "That's really flattering. I didn't realize you were a fan."

"I'm not a fan," she snaps. "And if I were I'd be pretty disappointed with your sorry performance on the floor tonight."

"Hey now." My grin slips. "You don't have to get personal. That's my career we're talking about."

She turns to leave, tossing the last words over her shoulder. "And this is mine."

I stand there like an idiot, thinking of all the ways I could arrange to meet her. I'm sure I'll see her on the regular from now on if she's assigned to this beat. I dry the last of the water from my aching body and pull on my T-shirt and sweats before I head to the hotel alone. I'm not worried that it didn't happen for Avery and me tonight.

Maybe I'm being cocky, but I'm sure it won't take long.

It never does.

TWO

Avery

Ten Years Later

"'M CONVINCED THE FUNDAMENTAL PROBLEM OF SOCIETY IS technology evolves much faster than the male brain."

I aim the words at my producer and best friend Sadie, meeting her eyes over my iPad.

"How else do you explain dick pic scandals?" I ask. "Something as simple as *not* sending pictures of your dick because it could cost you an election, a career, a marriage—men just cannot grasp. It's like this ancient urge to prove who has the bigger dick. Only instead of pissing on things, they send images of their penises into the ether."

I point to yet another post about my co-host's JunkGate. "I thought Gary was smarter than this."

Sadie walks to the desk and peers over my shoulder at the screen.

"I thought Gary was *bigger* than this," she says.

Our inelegant snorts meet in the quiet of my office.

"I had my suspicions." I set the iPad down and whirl my seat around a few times. "He's got that look small-dick men always have."

"What look do men with small dicks have?"

"Girl, if you've never seen it," I say, stopping my spinning chair long enough to offer a wry grin. "Count yourself lucky."

"As much as I'm enjoying all this girl talk at Gary's expense,"

Sadie says, dark eyes sobering in her pretty face. "We need to discuss what this means for *Twofer*."

"They're not firing him from the show, are they?" I stop grinning and grip the edge of my desk. "I mean, yeah. It's bad and indiscrete and embarrassing, but surely not a fire-able offense."

"No, not firing, but it does violate the conduct clause in his contract, and it's not his first time." Sadie leans back in the seat across from me, linking her hands over her stomach. "And it's definitely a distraction the show doesn't need, so they're suspending him for three weeks."

"I figured as much. I hope, for his sake, it was worth it." A rueful grin pulls one corner of my mouth back into humor briefly before uncertainty drags it back down. "So how will we handle his absence? Rotating guest hosts? Me solo?"

"Not solo. *Twofer's* popularity is built on the back and forth of opposing perspectives. We need a guest host, just while Gary's gone." Sadie shakes her head and leans forward to grab and munch some of the salted seaweed I was snacking on before she arrived. "This stuff tastes like literal shit. You're aware?"

"Focus. You can't just say I'm getting some guest host and not tell me who, like right away. Who is it?"

"Someone the audience will love tuning in to see."

"Who?"

"Someone credible."

"Who, Sadie?"

"Someone handsome."

"What's handsome got to do with journalism?"

Sadie slants me a knowing look. It's not just journalism. It's *television*, and looks mean a lot too often even in sports. I have enough firsthand experience with producers' requests and standards to understand the look she's giving me. When we first started the show two years ago, SportsCo executives asked me to "consider" pressing my hair for a more "polished" look and said they "loved my weight" just where it was. I doubt very seriously they had those conversations with my male co-host.

"Okay. You're right. Looks count," I concede. "So he's handsome. Who?"

"Retired. He's a future Hall of Famer," Sadie mumbles around a mouthful of the seaweed she insists is vile.

"Which sport?" I ask cautiously. Some retired athlete coming on my show who doesn't know jack shit about not just *playing* sports, but analyzing them, debating them, covering them is not what I need on set.

"We're playing ba-sket-baaaaaall," Sadie sings the famous Kurtis Blow refrain

and seesaws her shoulders.

Hmmm. Credible. Handsome. Basketball. Retired. Future Hall of Famer.

"No!" The word cannons from my mouth with fire power. "Not—"

"Mack Decker," Sadie finishes, her smile satisfied. "We got Mack Decker."

"Then un-get Mack Decker." I stand and pace, my go-to when something bothers me intensely, as the worn path in front of my desk attests. "He's arrogant, conceited, self-important—"

"Is this about that towel incident?" Sadie's evil grin hopes it is.

"That was ten years ago. Of course not."

Sadie's steady stare bores holes into my face.

"Okay, maybe a *very* little," I admit, rushing on over her laughter. "What professional athlete wearing a towel hits on a journalist in the locker room? Like, who does that?"

"You said yourself it was ten years ago."

"It was humiliating, and the guys on the beat teased me about it mercilessly. It took a long time for me to live that down." I stop pacing to face Sadie, digging in my heels literally and figuratively. "Besides, he may have been a professional athlete, but he's a novice commentator. No damn way I'm working with him."

"Okay, for real, *mami*?" Sadie tips her head, setting a shiny dark curtain of hair in motion. "You are all caps right now and I need you lower case."

"Isn't there someone else?" I perch on the end of the desk and kick my foot out to tap her knee. "Work with me here."

"No, there isn't." Sadie glares at the seaweed like it's compelling her to pop another strand of it in her mouth. "And I couldn't do anything to change this if I wanted to, which I don't."

"You're the producer. Of course, you have a say."

"Not in this one. Came from the very top." Sadie catches the heel of the shoe I'm banging against my desk. "Hey. It's a coup to have Deck co-hosting. He's been doing guest spots all season, and killing it. In addition to being a basketball genius, he's articulate and willing to learn. He may be new to commentating, but he's a natural on camera."

"I know," I admit grudgingly. "I've seen him."

"So what's the problem? I never heard much about the towel thing after the initial hoopla."

"No, they ended up reassigning me, and after the initial round of teasing, it died down." I extract my shoe from her grip and walk over to the window, no less impressed by the New York City view today than when I first landed this job and this office.

"Then I don't see the problem," Sadie says from behind me.

I don't face her and maybe I don't want to face myself.

There's always been a huge question mark over MacKenzie Decker. What would have happened if I had gone against my better judgment and taken him up on his offer of "or something"? What if I hadn't been reassigned from his team's beat? All I know of him has been through the news and by reputation over the years, but every time I hear his name . . . I don't know. Something stirs in me, and I'm not sure I'm quite ready for stirring.

So much has happened for us both, I know that encounter at his locker should be water long under the bridge. Deck won an MVP, two championships, and every award that counts. He got married. Divorced. Injured. Retired. I'm helming my own show on SportsCo, one of the biggest sports networks around. I was engaged. My brain short circuits before I go any further because I can't deal with all the *feelings* today. Not about my fiancé.

"You seem on edge. Is it . . ." Sadie's voice is careful in the way I've come to hate.

"Is it Will?"

She can be irritatingly clairvoyant at times.

"I'm fine." My mouth autopilots the words, a knee-jerk response to the question people have asked me a thousand times in a thousand different ways over the last year.

"If you need to—"

"I said I'm fine, Sade." I swivel a look over my shoulder that tells her not to push. For once she listens.

"Okay. Just saying I'm here. I know things have been—" Her mother's ring tone, Ricky Martin's "Livin' la Vida Loca," interrupts. "Hold on."

Thank God for Mama and Ricky Martin. This is the last thing I want to discuss.

"What, Ma?" Sadie asks, phone pressed to her ear.

That's the last English word from her mouth for the next five minutes since Sadie unleashes a torrent of Spanish to the woman on the other line. The only words I understand are "burrito" and "Atlanta Housewives."

I'm grateful for this brief reprieve from our conversation. Bad enough I have to work with Mack Decker. Now the feelings and memories that come with Will rise up and try to steal any peace, any confidence I've found.

"Yeah, yeah," Sadie says, easing back into English. "I'll tell her."

"Tell me what?" I demand, leaning my back against the cool glass of my window.

"How do you know she meant you?" Sadie lifts one perfectly threaded brow.

"She always means me. She loves me." I shrug. "What'd Ma say?"

"She wants you to meet my cousin Geraldo."

I chortle. That's the best way to describe the amused sound I make. I cover my mouth when Sadie glares at me.

"Sorry, Sade."

"Don't hate on my cousin, Avery."

"I'm sorry." A helpless laugh belies my apology. "As a journalist, how do you expect me to take a man named Geraldo seriously? Besides, you know I have no desire to date anyone."

"I know it's hard, and maybe it's too soon for an actual relationship," Sadie says, sympathy and determination all over her face. "But just meeting someone? That's not so bad. I just . . . you have to move on. And you never talk about it."

I swallow past the guilt clogging my throat and nod quickly, dismissively. I only talk about Will to my therapist. If you aren't charging me two hundred dollars an hour, these lips are sealed.

"You know I'm here if you need me," Sadie finally speaks softly and stands, nodding when my only response is a quick auto-smile. "Wanna grab something to eat?"

"Nah." I gesture to the open laptop planted in the spill of papers on my desk. "I got another couple hours of prep for tomorrow's show."

"Speaking of which, can you come in a little early to go over things with Decker?"

"He's starting *tomorrow*?" My mouth falls open and my heart starts running like a motor. "I can go one day without a co-host. Give me a day at least to get ready."

"You've had day-of host changes before," Sadie reminds me while she sways her hips to the door. "You're a professional. What's there to get ready for?"

Even after a decade, I still recall with perfect clarity the golden-brown hair, darkened and damp from his shower, curling at the nape of his strong neck. The chiseled landscape of chest and abs. The long legs, sculpted and bronzed extending beyond the small protective square of white terry cloth. I've only seen Mack Decker a handful of times over the years at awards shows, events, and the like. Usually he was with his wife and I was with Will. We were always cordial and polite, but somewhere deep in the secret corners of my heart, I allowed myself the tiniest bit of disappointment that he remained a question all these years. Sure, for a few weeks after the towel incident I was humiliated and offended and pissed off.

And flattered.

And intrigued.

And . . . turned on.

Three things I don't have time or space in my life for right now.

"It was ten years ago, Avery," I mumble, sitting in my chair to examine analytics for tomorrow's show.

Decker has always been an unanswered question. Bottom line under all my excuses, now that the opportunity may re-present itself, maybe I'm not ready for the answer.

THREE

Avery

MacKenzie Decker's arrogance is tailor-made, draped over him like one of his Armani suits. Fitted to his shoulders by years of fawning fans. Tapered to the broad, muscular back through a myriad of accolades, trophies, titles and championship rings. Perfectly fit to slide along the muscled length of his legs when he strides into SportsCo like he owns the place.

He *could* own the place. His net worth is no secret thanks to year after year on *Forbes* Highest Paid Athletes list. Most of his money comes from endorsements, not the lucrative NBA contracts he netted for twelve seasons. That smile. Those eyes. That body. His charm. Fifth Avenue served him up and Main Street feasted, making him a household name practically from the moment he was drafted.

He definitely doesn't need this job. Maybe that's what bothers me most.

He doesn't need this job. I do.

He didn't have to work to get here. I did.

Graduating at the top of my journalism class from Howard University, paying my dues on crowded sidelines, discarding modesty in locker rooms of naked men—I did whatever it took to get my own show. He just walks right in fresh from retirement like the party should start now that he's here. My show is just a pit stop between his storied career and the Hall of Fame. It grinds my teeth that he sits in the seat across from me like it's a throne. Like this is all his due and his kingdom. Like I'm his subject.

Yeah. That's what bothers me.

It better not be the way his presence sizzles in the air like hot oil tossed into a frying pan. It better not be his scent, clean and male with an undercurrent of lust. Or his amber-colored eyes surrounded by a wedge of thick lashes. It better not be any of those things because I had a talk with my body this morning, and we decided by mutual agreement that I would not respond physically to this man.

"Decker, welcome!" Sadie says, her smile unusually bright and her eyes slightly dazzled. "We're so glad to have you."

That slow-building smile starts behind his eyes, quirks his sinfully full lips and creases at the corners. We're roughly the same age. He's a little older, so he must be thirty-five, thirty-six or so by now, and the years have been oh so kind. If it hadn't been for a career-ending injury last year, he'd still be balling.

"I'm glad to be here." The voice, modulated and slightly southern, is that graveled rasp typically only earned by a few packs a day, except Decker is famously fastidious about what goes into his body, temple that it is. Nature just granted him that voice. I remind myself not to inspect all the other things nature awarded this man.

"You know Avery of course." The look Sadie turns on me holds a subtle threat in case I'm feeling froggy this morning. Lucky for her I had my cold brew coffee. That stuff keeps me out of jail. I'd hate to meet me without it.

I extend my hand, which he immediately enfolds in his. It's warm and huge. You forget how big these guys are when you watch them on television, but standing here in the well-toned flesh, Decker towers over me by at least a foot. He makes me feel small and delicate. I *love* feeling small and delicate . . . said no self-respecting sports reporter ever. Add that to the ever-growing list of things he makes me feel that I don't like.

"Good to see you again, Avery." He looks down at our hands still clasped.

"Yeah, you, too." I wiggle my fingers for him to let go, and for a moment mischief breaks through his neutral expression, before he releases me and sits at the conference room table.

"Thanks for stepping in, Deck," Sadie says. "How's the penthouse suite?"

SportsCo has a great relationship with the luxury hotel across the street, often holding events and putting up guests there. I'm assuming Deck is staying in the penthouse while he's with the show.

"It's great," Deck says. "Glad I don't have to commute from Connecticut every day."

"Well we wanted to make it easy for you. Let us know if you need anything." Sadie hands us both folders. "Now did you guys get my email with the rundown of today's show?"

When we both nod, Sadie dives into the details. I was prepared to be unimpressed. So many athletes assume because they played their sport, they know *all* sports and can just hop in front of a camera and it'll be fine. Deck obviously didn't make that assumption. He's prepared. And I've seen him commentate since he retired. He's good.

There's a studied ease to him, a carefully cloaked intensity. People can't always handle the passion it takes to do great things. I'm allergic to average and abhor mediocrity. That leaks into every aspect of my life. Type A. Driven. I'm not sure what you'd call it, but it's all over Mack Decker, too. He was renowned for it on the court, the alpha dog leading his pack to victory by any means necessary. As we review the elements of today's show, I look up more than once to find all of that intensity fixed on me. The dark gold stare pins me to my ergonomic leather seat. I make sure not to squirm, though it feels like, with nothing more than sex appeal and quiet tenacity, he's holding me hostage.

"All good?" Sadie looks between the two of us once we're done, but her query targets me. I know this because I know Sadie. I didn't want Decker stepping in, but even I can't deny his professionalism and competence. And obviously he'll be catnip for our viewers. Every excuse to *not* want him here keeps melting away. Eventually I'll have to deal with the real reason I've resisted him as a guest host.

But not yet.

"Yeah." I scribble nonsense on the pad in front of me, one of the many ways I exert my abundant nervous energy. "All sounds good to me."

Decker glances at the papers in front of him. "I'll try to keep it together in the last segment when Magic Johnson comes on set."

"What?" The word rides a laugh past my lips. "Are you serious?"

"I'm not allowed to lose my shit over the greatest point guard to ever lace up?" He leans back, lips twitching and arms crossed over the expanse of chest hidden beneath his crisp shirt.

"I'm glad you qualified *point* guard, not shooting guard, because we'd have a problem if you don't acknowledge Jordan as the Almighty Guard."

Decker's deep-timbered chuckle moves the muscles of his throat and slides over me like a lasso, roping me in and tugging me closer.

"I'm not having the Greatest of All Time debate with you, Avery."

"Good because there's no debate about who the GOAT is." I toss my pen on the table like a gauntlet. "You tell me anyone other than Jordan, we got a problem."

He expels a disdainful puff of air.

"Then we got a problem."

"Heresy." I lean forward, salivating for a good debate with a worthy opponent. "Who you got?"

He holds up three fingers. "Wilt, Kareem and Russell."

"Three!" Outrage drags the word from my mouth. "How can you have three ahead of Jordan? MJ at number four is just . . . I . . . I . . . just . . ."

"While she tries to gather her thoughts," Sadie interjects with a grin and a glance at her phone. "I gotta take this. Thanks again, Decker. Let's have a great first show."

When Sadie leaves, there's no buffer between me and the wall of
fine ass-ness that is MacKenzie Decker. It's the first time we've been
alone since he faced me naked in a roomful of laughing men a decade ago. I clear my throat needlessly since I have nothing to say. I felt
safe with Sadie as our chaperone. Now that it's just the two of us, I
can't remember what we were talking about with so much ease.

"You were saying?" Decker watches me expectantly.

"Huh?" I stall and blank-face him. "What was I saying?"

"Greatest of all time?" he prompts, anticipation brewing in his
eyes.

"I'll have to school you later." I force a smile, gathering the papers in front of me, tucking them into a neat stack and pressing them
to my chest. "I need to review some tape from last night's games before the show. See you on set."

I walk to the door and wave over my shoulder.

"I never got to apologize properly for the towel."

His words, injected seamlessly into our conversation, stunt my
steps. We were doing just fine until he had to go *there.*

"What?" I turn to consider him warily, half-hoping he'll let it go,
but there's no going back now. The polite façade has fallen away, baring his curiosity, his determined frankness.

"I said," he pauses deliberately to make sure I'm hearing him
clearly this time, "I never got to apologize properly for the towel. I
know there was some teasing on the circuit afterwards."

"It was a long time ago," I reply stiffly. "It's fine."

"I reached out, but I wasn't sure if—"

"I got the messages you left at the station." I keep my tone neutral and project confidence. "Thank you."

"But you never . . ." There's a trail of silence after his incomplete
thought.

"I was reassigned." I shift my feet and glance into the hall beyond the conference room, signaling that I'm ready to be done with
this conversation. "I knew we wouldn't see each other much, so . . ."

18

I leave a trail of my own, shrugging and hoping we can conclude this.

"Your hair used to be curly," he says, a grin accompanying yet another abrupt shifting of gears.

"Yes, well—"

"I liked it," he cuts in, stuttering my heartbeat and drifting a glance over my hair. "It's still beautiful this way."

He locks his whisky-tinted eyes with mine.

"You're still beautiful."

"Um, well, I—"

"We should grab a drink," he says, further disconcerting me. "*Or something.*"

He drops his words from that night on me, when he wore nothing but a tiny towel and super-size bravado.

Humor and irritation war inside me at the shared memory before I get them both under control.

"Look, Deck . . ." I shake my head and trap my bottom lip in my teeth before going on. "It's still a no."

He opens his mouth as if he has more to say, but my rigid expression must convince him he really shouldn't.

"Well, glad that's all behind us." The sorcerer smile, the one he must use to put people at ease, reappears. "I'll let you go prepare. See you on set."

I nod and turn on my heel, making sure to keep my steps steady and measured, even though I want to run back to my office before he decides to press the advantage I don't want him to know he has.

FOUR

Decker

THERE'S SOMETHING ABOUT AVERY HUGHES THAT RUBS ME THE RIGHT way.

She gets me worked up. It starts, as with most men, in my pants, but in no time it reaches my *other* head, the one with the brain, and it's her wit and sharp intelligence, her drive that keeps me wanting more. Even if there hadn't been all the ribbing after the towel incident, I still would have thought about her for days after we met. She's the kind of woman who makes an impression and lingers in your memory.

I last saw her about two years ago at a *Sports Illustrated* party. I'd been injured that season, and was pretty sure my NBA career was over. Even though my wife Tara stood at my side, glittering and clinging possessively, we both knew our marriage was over, too. It had been on life support for a while. We were scheduled to present a check from my charitable foundation that night, so we had to attend together, but we'd already filed the papers. Still, when I spotted Avery across the room with her fiancé, guilt chewed through my gut because I wanted to walk away from my soon-to-be-ex, snatch Avery from that dude and take her to some corner; pick up where we'd left off in that locker room.

It feels like I've lived a dozen lives since then. Seasons in the NBA should be measured like dog years. Not just the wear and tear on your body, but the wear and tear on your soul. Greedy people, shattered hopes, broken marriages.

Missed chances.

Avery feels like the biggest missed chance of all. Maybe she retained that mystery because I never got to know her. Never got to taste her. That night at the *SI* party, when our glances collided across eight years and a crowded room, I had to accept that I never would. I had only seen her a handful of times and from a distance since our first meeting, but in a moment, before she had time to disguise it, her unguarded expression told me she hadn't forgotten. That I was still . . . something, even if it was just an annoying, awkward memory. Avery, being the consummate professional, contorted her lips into a plastic smile and turned back to the man at her side.

Only that man hasn't been at her side the last few months. Lately, the few times I watched her show, the ring she wore that night was gone. I'm not sure what's happened, but the ring's not there now, and I'm assuming . . . okay, *hoping* . . . the man is gone, too.

When SportsCo called about subbing as Avery's co-host on *Twofer*, I cancelled whatever my team had lined up to make it happen. This could get interesting . . . if Avery would let it.

If she would let *me*.

We're a week in, and on camera, Avery and I have a natural connection that viewers are loving, but she's kept me at a polite distance otherwise. When the lights go down, her guard goes up, and she presents that phony, careful neutrality she thinks will keep me out. But every day, I see a new crack in that wall she hides behind, and it only stokes my curiosity to see what's in there. It's time to chip away at the wall. Time to be the hammer.

I study her during our production meeting. She's making a point to the team about a camera angle. An image of her pinned against the conference room door highjacks my imagination; my tongue plunged so deeply down her throat she'd have to beg for breath. Of me sliding to my knees and pushing that skirt past her thighs, pulling her legs onto my shoulders and roughly shoving her panties aside. Of my mouth open and worshiping between her legs. Of my face wet from her passion gushing onto me.

Puppies. Ice cream. Old people fucking.

I mentally run through the list that usually keeps a hard-on at bay, but it's not working this time, and my dick is a pipe in my pants. I would handle this woman. I would pick her up when I kiss her. Literally sweep her off her feet and hold her by the ass. Show her what it feels like to be kissed suspended in the air. I'd press her against me so she felt how much I wanted her. Until she felt my erection and had to deal with it. Until she had to deal with *me*. I scoot my chair another inch under the table, struggling to rein in this fantasy.

Puppies. Ice cream. Old people fucking.

If this woman is indifferent to me, I'll eat both my championship rings. I made my living reading plays and picking apart defenses. From my experience, people and relationships aren't much different, and there's no way I misread the attraction between us that badly. She's not a woman you can rush, but I only have two weeks left on my guest stint before good ol' dick pic returns. With so little time left on the clock, I think this calls for the full-court press. End-to-end coverage. Man-to-man defense . . . or in this case, man-to-woman. No letting up until the opponent is worn down. I live for this shit. No one can beat me at this game.

"Does that sound good?" Avery interrupts my inner pep talk, long-lashed eyes blinking at me over the cup of cold brew I've been bringing her every day.

What the hell are we talking about?

I glance around the conference room, packed with the crew for the production meeting. Everyone's watching me expectantly.

"Deck?" Avery asks with a tiny frown. "I said does that sound good?"

"Hmmmm . . ." I scrunch my face like I'm pondering the subject really hard, hoping she'll elaborate.

"I mean, if you want to do the Holiday predictions last instead," she continues. "We totally can."

"Nah." *Ah! The Holiday predictions. Right.* "We can leave it at the top."

She tilts her head and narrows her eyes. "You mean in the middle?"

"Middle, yeah." I nod sagely. "Perfect place for it."

"Well if we're all agreed," Sadie says, closing her laptop. "That's a wrap."

Everyone starts dispersing. I'll find some reason to linger until Avery finishes the discussion she's having with one of the show's writers.

"Don't worry," Sadie whispers to me while she finishes packing her things. "She's coming, too."

If I take my eyes off Avery for even a second, she might dart off. That woman has become really good at avoiding me. I spare Sadie a quick glance to figure out what she's even talking about.

"Coming where?" I ask. "Who?"

"You really *were* checked out." She laughs, shaking her head and shoving her phone into her purse. "Sorry if we bore you with the details of planning the show."

"It's not personal." I do an Avery check—still chatting—before looking back to Sadie. "I hate meetings. Always have, and my mind tends to drift. So, who's going where and what's up?"

"We're all going to grab drinks and dinner."

No, thanks.

"I don't think I'll—"

"And Avery's coming with us," Sadie cuts in with a knowing look.

Oh, well in that case.

"Man's gotta eat." She and I share a conspiratorial grin. "What gave me away?"

"Um, what *didn't*?" Sadie leans against the conference room table. "Bringing her coffee every day. Not leaving any room until she does. The way you—"

"All right, all right." I glance around self-consciously to see if anyone heard her spouting how whipped I've been behaving. "So, what do I do about it, since you know so much?"

"*Do* about it?" Her smile is just relishing the novel positon I'm in having to chase a woman.

"I didn't think I'd ever have a shot. She was wearing some other guy's ring the last time I saw her. I don't want to waste my chance this time."

The humor on Sadie's face fades, her eyes go sober.

"Oh, Deck. You don't know."

"Don't know what?"

Before she can enlighten me, Avery walks up and Sadie's mouth snaps shut and her eyes stretch with some silent warning I'm clueless about.

"What's with all the lollygagging?" Avery asks, playfully bumping Sadie's shoulder, her mouth stretched into a wide grin. "We eating or what?"

I wish she'd be that easygoing with me. Despite our chemistry onscreen, I can barely get her alone long enough to have a decent conversation.

"I was just telling our friend here he should come with us." Sadie smiles up at me. "Right, Deck?"

Avery's grin slips, but she recovers quickly enough to offer me a polite, if stiff, smile.

"You should," she tells me. "This place does a great dirty martini, and I love their steak."

I rarely drink and gave up red meat years ago.

"Two of my favorite things," I lie. "What are we waiting for?"

The prospect of a few extra hours to crack her tough outer shell has my blood humming through my veins like it's pre-game and I'm facing an especially challenging opponent.

We're all crowded in the elevator on our way down, and I meet the guarded interest in Avery's eyes I've become accustomed to over the last week. Not an opponent. I think we're on the same team. I think we want the same thing. She just doesn't know it yet.

FIVE

Avery

TWO OF HIS FAVORITE THINGS, MY ASS.

Decker ignored the steaks, went straight for the pan roasted sea bass, and has been drinking water all night.

I take a long, grateful sip of my second martini, thanking God for whomever had the foresight to invent them. It's a massage, a hot bath and an orgasm all shaken and stirred into one delightfully numbing concoction. And the closer we get to Christmas, the more numb I need to be.

"You look like you're enjoying that," Decker says, pushing his plate away.

"And it looks like you *didn't* enjoy that." I nod toward his half-eaten fish.

"No, it was delicious. I just wasn't as hungry as I thought I was."

"And you decided to forego the alcohol, too? Even though martinis and steak are your faves?" I shouldn't toy with him, but it's kind of fun watching a man so notoriously pursued by women making excuses to spend time with *me*, even though I'm not exactly sure what he wants.

Scratch that.

The barely concealed lust steaming in his eyes tells me what he wants. Problem is, I think I might want it, too, but I can't. If my vagina was the only thing I had to worry about, this would be a no-brainer. Six feet and seven inches of tanned, beautiful *man*. What's there to think about? But even just in our first week working together, I've seen a depth to him I didn't expect. The same determination and commitment to excellence that has him Hall of Fame-bound, he's applied to guest hosting. TV's a steep learning curve, and I gotta give it to him. He's doing a great job. He's funny, sharp, thinks on his feet, and can talk any other sport almost as easily as he can basketball. For most women that wouldn't be a turn on, but for me? Yeah, very much so. With a man like Decker, the vajayjay isn't the only body part to consider. He could endanger my heart, and that troubled organ still hasn't recovered from Will.

"So, seems like we have pretty much opposite picks for every prediction," Decker says, leaning back in his seat.

"Prediction?" I snap out of my own thoughts and tune into our conversation. "What do you mean?"

"For the Holiday Picks segment." Decker lifts his brows, waiting for me to catch up. "For next week's show."

"Oh, yes," I deadpan, warming to a subject I'm comfortable discussing. "Shocking that we're at odds."

"I know, right?" He leans forward to rest his elbows on the table and turns his body toward me, effectively blocking out the rest of the table. "We both have the Wolves and the Sabers going to the NCAA Championship, but I have the Wolves winning. You picked the Sabers."

"Yeah, because Caleb Bradley and the Sabers took it last year," I remind him. "What makes you think they won't do it again?"

"August West makes me think they won't do it again. If West hadn't sprained his ankle last year, he could have taken it then. He's got that killer instinct."

"If we're both right and they both advance, it'll be one helluva final no matter who comes out on top."

"It'll be West. Mark my words. I recognize a champ in the making when I see one. Caleb Bradley may be the All-American Golden Boy, but August is the one to watch."

His smile is smug, but I can't help smiling in return. It's basketball. I know my shit, but he's *lived* it and has two championships to show for the years he put into the League.

"Who am I to disagree? You *are* the future Hall of Famer." My sarcasm delivers the compliment backhanded.

"Don't you forget it," he replies with a chuckle.

"Did you always know you wanted to play ball?" I shock myself by asking. I don't do lengthy conversations with this man. Or at least I haven't over the last week. This martini must be dirtier than I thought. It's going to my head. As long as it doesn't start heading south, we should be okay.

"Always." He shrugs. "Honestly it could have gone either way. Basketball or football. I had looks for both."

"You were scouted for both sports? College?"

"Yeah, I played both even through high school, but it came to the point I had to choose."

"What position did you play? Football, I mean, obviously." Everyone knows he's one of the greatest point guards to ever play basketball.

"What do you think I played?" He props his chin in his hand, the bourbon-flavored eyes brimming with curiosity. About me.

"Hmmm." I tip my head and squint one eye, assessing. "Your leadership skills are off the chart."

"Well thank you." He dips his head and smiles to acknowledge the compliment.

"You don't follow others well."

His smile falters, and he glares at me, even though there's still humor in his eyes.

"You always think you know best," I continue, enjoying this more by the second. "And you love ordering people around."

"Okay, maybe I should just tell you before you really hurt my feelings."

"Like I could," I scoff.

He doesn't answer, but looks down at the table, a smile curling the corners of his wide, sensual mouth.

"Quarterback," I say triumphantly. "Am I right?"

His laugh is richer than the chocolate ganache I ordered, but shouldn't eat.

"God, I wish I could say you're wrong," he admits with a grin. "Yeah, quarterback."

"I knew it." I brush my shoulders off.

"Uh huh. Now who's the know it all?"

"Oh, I don't deny it." I take a sip of my neglected drink. "I always assume I have the right answer."

"I have observed that over the last week." He shoots me a speculative glance before continuing. "There's a lot I haven't learned, though."

The vodka seems to pause midway down my throat. I cough a little and wait for him to start the questions I've seen in his eyes for days.

"Like did you play any sports yourself?" he asks.

I breathe a little easier. This is comfortable territory.

"Track and field."

"Ahhh." He nods as if answering himself. "That explains it."

"Explains what?" I ask, taking another sip.

His eyes burn a trail over my neck and breasts until the table interrupts his view.

"Your body."

I cough again, reaching for a napkin to wipe my mouth.

"My-my body?" I hate how breathy I sound all of a sudden. With a few well-placed words and a look, he has me sputtering and simmering.

"I'm sure you know women who run track and field often develop a certain body type," he says, leaning forward until I can't see much of anything beyond the width of his shoulders. "Lean arms."

Even though my arms are hidden beneath my blouse, my skin

heats up when he runs his eyes over them.

"Muscular legs," he continues, locking his eyes with mine. "A tight, round—"

"I'm aware," I cut in, "of what my body looks like. I see it every day."

"Wish I could say the same."

My face heats up. I know a blush doesn't show through my complexion, but judging by the way his grin goes wider and wickeder, it doesn't take color in my cheeks to tell him I'm heating up.

"So, you chose basketball." I shift the conversation back to safer ground that won't burn under my feet like hot coals.

"Yes." His grin lingers, but he indulges my redirection. "All through college."

"And then the NBA," I add.

"Yeah, if you work hard as hell and sacrifice just about everything else in your life, dreams really do come true." He grimaces. "At least some of them do."

I heard about his divorce, but don't want to assume that's what he means. He glances up, a wry twist to his lips.

"You wear your questions all over your face, Avery."

I huff a short laugh. "Do I?"

"I did have a dream other than basketball, if you're curious." His shoulders lift and fall, but they seem to be lifting more weight than he lets on. "I wanted a wife, kids, the whole package."

"And you got them, right?" I ask softly.

I want to ask what went wrong. I wonder if that question is on my face, too, because he answers without me voicing it.

"Tara, my ex, and I didn't as much grow apart, as we never should have been together."

I've thought that of Will and me many times. Wondered if things would have ended differently if he'd never met me. Sometimes it keeps me up at night. Sometimes it's the first thing I think about when I wake up.

"Statistically, half of all married couples would say the same thing." I smile my sympathy. "And kids? I heard you had a daughter."

"Yeah, my little girl Kiera." The rugged lines of his face noticeably soften. "You wanna see?"

I nod, surprisingly eager to see how his DNA played out on a little female face.

"Oh, she's so pretty, Deck," I whisper, my eyes glued to his phone screen. She's blonde and looks uncannily like the woman I saw Decker with at a *Sports Illustrated* party a couple of years ago. Her eyes, though, are golden brown, just like her father's. I glance up from the phone.

"She has your eyes."

"That's about it." He chuckles, accepting his phone and glancing affectionately at the picture before setting it on the table. "I can't take much credit for how beautiful she is."

I look away, afraid my eyes would betray my thoughts as clearly as he said he could see them. Afraid he'll see that I think he's the most beautiful specimen I've ever encountered. That sometimes during the show, I almost lose my train of thought wondering how his tawny hair would feel wrapped around my fingers. That in just a week, I've memorized the curve of his mouth and how he smells. Not his cologne, but that rawer scent made from nothing but skin and bone and him that rests just below the veneer of civilization we all wear.

"Tara just moved to LA," Decker continues, a rueful set to his lips. "And took Kiera with her."

"I'm sorry." I frown. "It must be harder to see her now with you still on the East Coast, I guess?"

"Yeah. Takes a little more work, but she's worth it. I've accomplished a lot, but she's the best thing I've ever done." He shrugs and then turns an inquisitive look on me. "What about you?"

"What about me?" My fingers tighten around the fragile stem of my martini glass. My heart tightens in my chest, braced for questions I'll have to evade.

"Well, I know you were engaged," he says with a careful look at my bare ring finger. "And I don't think you are anymore."

He doesn't know.

I savor that tiny slice of time while I can where he doesn't know. For the last year of my life, everyone has known what happened. And I often feel smothered under the weight of their speculation, their awkward sympathy, their damn good intentions because they know everything. Well, they *think* they know everything. I have my secrets; secrets kept alive only by me because only Will knew.

And now Will is gone.

"He died." I clear my throat, my lips trembling in the most vexing way. I steady them like I've learned to steady my emotions. "Will, my fiancé, died last year around this time actually."

When I say *everyone* knows, it's not like when "everyone" knows Deck got a divorce or the details of a multimillion-dollar contract he inked. When "everyone" knows what's going on in his life, it's the world. His fame is much broader than mine. I'm a sportscaster, and I'm on television, but my life isn't national news, much less international. With Deck, the whole world could know his business. The whole world doesn't know my fiancé died last December. Only everyone who knows me and everyone who knew Will. Everyone in my life knows. And now so does Decker.

For the last few minutes, it was easy to forget that just beyond the barrier of Deck's torso and shoulders, our colleagues are drinking and talking. Laughing and blowing off steam after a long day. I didn't realize how completely Deck had managed to isolate us; to monopolize me until it gets so quiet in our little corner.

"Avery, I'm so sorry." His voice is a soft rumble of compassion. "I had no idea. I hadn't heard."

I nod, panicking as a familiar knot ignites inside my throat, threatening to choke me. Out of habit and necessity, I start blinking rapidly against ill-timed tears.

"Yeah, it wasn't . . . something we broadcast." Dark humor taunts the corner of my mouth. "Will would have hated that; to be a part of some media circus. He wasn't . . . he was the last one to draw attention to himself."

A door cracks open that I keep closed and locked; that I try to forget exists. The one with all my memories of Will. His smile, which had become so rare at the end. It was the first thing I liked about him; that his smile was kind and genuine. I can't do this. Not here. Not now. Not with Decker watching my face for signs of distress. If he keeps looking, he'll find it. It's not as deeply buried as I manage to convince most people. Decker isn't most people, and I instinctively know he won't be fooled.

"It's getting late." My smile is a cold, waxy curve trying its best to look alive. "I think I'll go."

"Avery," he says softly. Just that. Just my name, but there's so much more there, and I can't do this shit right now.

I ignore him and reach down to grab my purse, using those few seconds to compose myself and swipe at the corners of my eyes. When I stand, so does he. Our eyes clash for a moment, mine watery and his concerned. I step around him, snapping the thread strung taut between us, and address my coworkers.

"Okay, guys." I spread a bright smile around to everyone. "I'm heading out. Have a good weekend."

Blindly, I make my way to the door, longing for the fresh air, at least as fresh as New York City has to offer.

"Hey, Ave," Sadie calls from behind me when I'm just a few feet away from the exit. "Wait up."

I stop and turn, smoothing my expression into patient inquiry, hoping the churning waves in my gut aren't washing up on my face.

"You okay?" Sadie sees more than most. She knows more than most, too, but even she doesn't know everything.

"I'm fine." I roll my eyes when she gives me the look that says *it's me you're talking to.* "Okay. I'm not exactly fine, but I will be."

"Do you need—"

"I just need to go home, Sade." There's a pleading note in my voice that I can't suppress much longer. "Please. Just let me get out of here."

Sadie nods, hooks her arm around my neck and whispers into my ear.

"It's gonna get better, babe."

Some things don't. Some things never get better because they can never be undone. I had to learn that for myself the hardest way. I won't try to teach Sadie at the hostess stand of this nice restaurant.

"Night," I settle for saying before walking swiftly to the door.

I draw in great lungfuls of the cold night air and start walking. With every step, my heart decelerates and my breath evens and my tears dry up. That's all I needed. Some time to myself.

"Avery!" a deep voice calls from behind me.

So much for time to myself.

I turn to find Decker almost caught up to me, his long legs making quick work of the few feet separating us. I wanted to be alone, and he's ruining that. Yet my heart lifts a little at the sight of him. I knew it! If my vagina and my heart ever get on the same page, they'll be my downfall.

"Can you not take a hint?" My voice lacks the irritation it should hold.

"Only the ones I want to take," he replies easily, hunching into his dark coat and squinting against the cold. "You walking?"

"Obviously since you're walking to catch me."

"Ahhh." He grins, slanting me an amused look. "The smartass is back."

My answering smile dims as I remember what chased me out of the restaurant in the first place.

"I meant are you walking all the way home?" he asks.

"It's not far." I glance up at him. "And I don't need an escort."

"Well you got one, lady."

I roll my eyes, which only makes him laugh. We're silent for the next few steps, and I focus on the bustling anonymity of the city. You can get lost in this hectic, harried press of humanity. I have over the last year. I've hidden myself in its crevices and I've hurt in my solitude. I thought it was what I deserved—to hurt alone. With Decker here, the sounds of the city swallowing up the yawning silence inside of me, I wonder if maybe I've been wrong. It feels good to have some-one . . . here. Just here. Not demanding answers, or hovering for fear I'll self-destruct. But someone who just wants my company and wants to offer theirs. It dents my loneliness.

"Here I am." I stop in front of my apartment building and turn to Deck, prepared to say good-bye.

Of course, he walks ahead to the entrance. My doorman recog-nizes him instantly, rushing over to hold the glass doors wider for him.

"Deck, we sure miss seeing you on the court," he says, an eager grin splitting his face.

"Can't say I miss being out there as much as I thought I would," Decker replies, signing the slip of whatever paper the doorman found for his autograph. "I like not aching and creaking half the year. Eighty-two games for twelve years will kick your ass."

"Not to mention playoffs in the post-season," the doorman re-minds him with an admiring grin.

"Yeah, there were a few of those, too, huh?" Decker laughs and turns when the elevator arrives. "Nice meeting you."

"Great meeting you, too. Thanks for the autograph. My son'll love this. Good night, Ms. Hughes," the doorman adds, finally ac-knowledging me.

I return his smile, not minding being ignored. It's not every day you see a living sports legend. I remember feeling that way the first night I met Decker, even though I still had to ask him tough ques-tions. He'd won rookie of the year the season before and was already one of the brightest stars in the League. Remembering the towel inci-dent makes me smile as we get off the elevator.

"What are you grinning about?" Deck asks, narrowing his eyes in false suspicion. "I don't trust you when you grin like that."

Feeling a little lighter, I turn to face him, walking backward toward my door.

"I was thinking about the first night we met."

"Ugh." He shakes his head and closes his eyes briefly. "I was such an immature asshole."

"I think I told you that then." I laugh when he glowers at me. "You just admitted it. I'm agreeing with you. Be happy."

"You know it's funny. That was ten years ago." His smile as we keep walking borders on wistful, if such firm lips could be described that way. "So it feels like I've known you forever, but before I started the show last week, we'd never had a real conversation. I mean, unless you count the one at my locker."

"I don't." I lean against the door to my apartment. "You were wearing a towel, and not even that at one point."

"Nice." He stops in front of me. "I'll never live that down with you, will I?"

"Do you really want to?"

"Nope," he admits with a shameless, cocksure grin. "At least I knew you would never forget me."

As if I could.

I don't say the words, but something on my face must confess that I never forgot him. That sometimes in quiet moments alone, he was always an unanswered question. Or maybe I was afraid to ask. His humor evaporates, and his eyes take on that fierce focus I'd always noted when I watched him play. The camera would catch this exact look on his face; like the prize is in sight, and it was only a matter of four quarters before his opponent would yield. I wonder which quarter we're in.

"So, like I was saying." He picks up where he left off, that intense stare like steam hovering over my skin. "I feel like I've learned a lot about you since I started with the show."

"Is that right?" I press my shoulders into the door for support because that look is melting my bones, and I need to stand my ground.

"I know that as soon as you walk into a room, you charge the air," he says softly. "Everything comes to attention around you."

My breath stutters and I lick dry lips.

"I know that people enjoy following you so much they don't even realize you're leading them," he continues, taking a step closer and stealing another ounce of air from my lungs. "And that you're usually the smartest person in the room, but you know when to let other people think they are."

I thought butterflies in your stomach were some urban myth from Harlequin romance novels, but sure enough, something is fluttering in my belly at his words.

Aw, crap. I don't do butter fucking flies.

"And I know that as much as you light up onscreen, there's something sad in your eyes, and I hate it." He steps as close as he can, cups my cheek, locking our eyes. "I saw it tonight and I hate it, Avery."

He flattens his other hand against the door, his arms making an intimate alcove I couldn't escape if I wanted to.

I don't want to.

He pulls back just enough to search my face. Surely he sees my bottom lip trapped between my teeth because I must resist yielding to the warm comfort of him.

"I want to make it better, Ave," he whispers, the cool mint of his breath breezing over my lips. "I just want to . . ."

He scans my face, waiting for some sign from me that it's okay. That the desire to kiss me so clearly telegraphed in his eyes is okay. I can't find words to articulate that in this maelstrom of grief and desire and confusion, the only thing clear, the only thing that makes any sense right now, is for him to kiss me. So I don't say a word. I just lean forward until our lips meet.

SIX

Decker

SOFT AND FRESH LIKE PETALS.

I'm a jock. Not a dumb one, but a jock nonetheless. I don't describe a woman's lips as soft and fresh or compare a kiss to flowers. Besides the few years I was married to Tara, if it opened its legs and said yes or please, I fucked it. I always rushed it. A man's got needs, but I got in and I got out. This woman, this kiss, I have to savor. I'd be a fool not to. It's a first kiss. I understand the difference now between the first time you kiss someone, and a *first kiss*. This is a discovery of tongues and lips and heat. An introduction of our souls, if that doesn't sound too pussy-ish. It's how I feel, though. Like as our lips brush back and forth, as our tongues tangle, as I taste her, mouthful by delicious mouthful, I'm learning her secrets. I'm telling her mine. My hand slides from the door to flatten into the warmth of her back through the silk blouse, bringing her incrementally closer. The air shifts and takes the shape of lust; assumes the form of want. The sound of her moaning, the slight lift and fall of her breasts against my chest, testifies that she feels it, too.

The elevator dings, and our bodies go still even as we keep exchanging breaths and heartbeats through our clothes; even though my mouth is still poised above hers. I have her against the door, and every curve of her body is impressing itself on me, making sure I'll never forget how right we fit together. I look over my shoulder toward the elevator. The doors open, but no one gets off. That interruption was enough to bring her back to her senses, though. God knows I can't find mine.

"Um . . . you should go," she whispers, a muscle rippling along the smooth line of her jaw.

I bend to breathe over her mouth, so she can taste our kisses lingering on my lips. "Or you could invite me in."

Her scent and the warmth of her body take my senses hostage. I smell her and want to kiss her again so badly it stings my taste buds. Her eyes already regret the last few moments I thought were so perfect. I can't calm my emotions or my body that quickly.

"You don't want to come in, Deck."

"I assure you I do," I tell her.

A short laugh, deceptively light, breezes past her lips. She glances down to the floor and shakes her head.

"I'd make the worst one-night stand ever," she says.

"One-night stand?" I take her chin in hand and lift, forcing her to look at me. "I've waited a long time for this path to be clear. No conflict of interest. No other people standing in our way. I don't know exactly what I want, Avery, but it's damn sure more than one night."

If anything, my assurance that it's more than just physical, more than just a night to me, lights panic in her eyes.

"Oh, that's worse." She frowns even as she sends a sad smile up at me. "I'm not anywhere near ready for something like that, Deck."

She's not a tall woman, though the strength of her personality makes you forget that. I've easily got a foot or more and a hundred pounds on her. She tucks a shiny chunk of dark hair behind her shoulder, exposing the intricate whorl of her ear, the fine angle of her jaw. She acts tough. Hell, she *is* tough, but her fiancé died only a year ago. That would leave anyone kind of fragile. Of course, she's not ready. Up this close, invading her space, past the outer wall, I see the vulnerability; the desolation and pain. It stabs me in the chest.

"I get that," I say, my voice rough. "I'm so sorry about him, Ave. About your fiancé."

She nods, the tumult churning inside evident on her face. The need to comfort her has my hand up, palming her cheek and my other hand at her waist, pulling her into me. After a hesitation, she surrenders to it. Her forehead drops to my chest, and a ragged breath shudders through her slim body. The air thickens with lingering grief. She doesn't cry, but the dip of her shoulders, the tension of her body, broadcasts how difficult this still is. My hand traces a soothing path from between her shoulders to the small of her back, and I don't say anything, but leave her to take any comfort she can from the human contact. After a few moments, she shifts.

"Thanks, Deck," she says softly, pulling back. My hand tightens at her waist, anchoring her to me, despite the gap between our bodies. She feels so good, I'm not ready to relinquish her.

"I need to go." She stares at the button on my shirt instead of at me.

I'm about to refuse; to press the issue of the connection I know she feels, too, but there is just enough shadow in her dark eyes; trace amounts of the grief that brought us into each other's arms in the first place, to change my mind. My hand drops, and she turns to unlock her apartment door.

"I'll see you on set Monday." Her eyes meet mine cautiously like she thinks I might grab her.

That could happen.

"Sure." I step back. "Should be a great show."

Once she's safely inside, I board the elevator. She's right. Tonight wasn't the night. Based on what I learned about her fiancé, I can respect that. But after tasting her, not just her sweetness, but her tears, I know this is just clemency. She wants time. I can give her space, but I'm not giving up.

SEVEN

Avery

*H*AVE YOURSELF A MERRY LITTLE *C*HRISTMAS
Let your heart be light
From now on your troubles will be out of sight
I wake up with Will's favorite Christmas song in my head and my hand between my legs.

Sad and horny. That's what I am. I literally cannot remember the last time I had sex. I know it was with Will because I never cheated on him in the years we were together, but our sex life was so sporadic at the end, I can't recall the last time we made love. I need to get drunk and I need to get laid. I'm hoping at least one of those will happen tonight at the SportsCo Christmas party, but it probably won't be the latter. I told Decker the truth. I'd be an awful one-night stand, and if I were in the market for one, it wouldn't be at my office Christmas party. I've never dated colleagues or athletes, and that's pretty much the extent of tonight's guest list. Will was into advertising. He could barely tell a touchdown from a homerun. I liked that he had nothing to do with sports or my career. I needed something separate from the frenetic pace of television and the crazy news cycle I'm always enslaved to.

"God, Will." I stare up at the ceiling, fresh, hot tears rolling into my ears and soaking my hairline. "Why did you do it? *How* could you do it?"

I told Decker last night that Will died, but I didn't tell him it was at his own hand.

I've been through grief counseling. I see my therapist every week. I've read about suicide and depression and know all the statistics. Seventy-five percent of suicides are men. Statistically they follow through on their attempts at higher rates. Those stats spike during the holidays. All the signs were there, but I missed them. Ignored them? Denied them? I don't know how I lived with this man and wore his ring for two years, but never knew this morbid wish was growing inside of him, a dark bud I didn't even know had taken root.

And every morning for the last year, I woke up with one question on my lips.

Why?

"The last year," I repeat, my voice an early morning croak. "Oh, my God."

He's been gone a year today. I can't believe it, and in many ways, I feel as lost as I did the night he died.

There's a call I need to make. One I dread, but know I cannot avoid.

When it rings and rolls into voice mail, I hesitate. I could call back later, but I'm not sure I can handle it today, hearing the pain in his mother's voice. I'm ashamed to feel relief that Mrs. Hattfield doesn't answer. Even more ashamed that I take the coward's way out and leave a message.

"Hi, Mrs. H," I say after the beep. "It's me, Avery."

I pause, the right words eluding me while I squeeze the cell phone like it's the only thing anchoring me.

"I . . . um . . . I know today is difficult for you." I shove the words that feel so trite out of my mouth. "It's difficult for me, too. I can't imagine . . . I just . . ."

My voice evaporates for a moment.

"I miss him," I whisper, biting my lips against a sob and pressing my eyes closed to hold onto the last image I have of him. The deathly peace he'd taken for himself.

And it's true. I miss the guy I knew before; the one who went down on one knee at dinner and promised me forever. I even miss the sullen man who lived in the shadows the last part of his life. I'd take Will any way I could get him just to look in his eyes, grab his hands and beg him not to do it. For me. For his mother. For *himself*, to reconsider living.

"I hope you're not alone today." I take a second to compose myself before going on. "I know the next few weeks will be hard, Christmas will be hard without him."

I run one hand through my hair, frustrated that I don't have the right words and have nothing more to say.

"Okay, well, call me when you get this message," I say into the mechanical silence. "Talk to you soon."

Losing a child, it's the worst thing. When a child chooses to forfeit the very life you gave him, the pain must weigh even more. I wonder if she stares up at the ceiling some mornings asking *why* the way I do. Do her pain and grief cohabitate with a stewing rage? Does she want to drag him from the grave and shake him and call him a coward? I hate even thinking these things, but not acknowledging them to myself and at least to my therapist was ruining me. I don't know if these thoughts make me a bad person, but I know they make me sad. And frustrated. And helpless.

In my closet, I consider the row of beautiful dresses I could wear tonight. The last thing I want to do is go to a Christmas party, much less one Mack Decker is attending. Those moments at my door two weeks ago have been a source of torture. It wasn't just a reminder to my body what it's been missing, but to my emotions. That just beyond my comfort zone there may be solace for, not just my body, but for my soul.

What was I thinking? Letting him hold me? Letting him see my vulnerability? Those moments of letting go, resting against the solidity of him; being comforted by his heart beating just beyond the wall of his chest, were some of the sweetest I've had in a year. It was intoxicating, and I have no intention of getting drunk on him. He'd go straight to my head. Straight to my heart and between my legs, and I'm not ready for any of that.

I press my thighs together against a tide of want when I recall the moments that simmered between us. Waking up thinking about Will, and getting wet knowing I'll see Deck in a few hours—it feels so wrong, but at least I'm feeling. I haven't allowed myself to want a man since Will died. Maybe no one appealed to me the way Decker does, but he's the first one to punch holes in the fence around me.

I return to my selections for the party. I've worn the black dress to several office functions. It's flattering and conservative. It's the classic "little black dress" that goes everywhere and can serve many purposes. I touch the silky material of my other option. It's a dress made of sunsets, a glorious blend of gold and red, and it still bears the tags. I've never worn it. The deep V neckline is outdone by the deeper V that bares my back. The bottom is narrow and tight and will be a testament of all the squats I've done, though my ass is mostly genetics and years of track and field. My mother and aunts have never done squats a day in their lives, and you could bounce a quarter off their butts. As good as I know the dress will look, I'm still not sure I'll wear it. It's a statement dress, and knowing Decker will be there tonight, I'm not quite sure what I want to say.

EIGHT

Decker

"**S**O WHAT'S NEXT?"

The question catches me a little off guard. With a Jack and Coke halfway to my mouth, I pause to study Mike Dunlov, one of SportsCo's most popular anchors.

"I mean now that your co-hosting gig's up," he clarifies.

"Little bit of this," I answer flatly because I'm giving this guy nothing. "Little bit of that."

I toss back a portion of the much-needed drink. Playing pro ball allowed me to indulge many vices. I've had more pussy than any man has a right to in one lifetime, for example. I'm practically abstemious, though, when it comes to alcohol and what I eat. Always have been. This body was my lottery ticket, and I took care of it. But tonight, this liquor is a lifeline. It's been a bitch of a day. Mainly because my ex is being a bitch. Bad enough she moved my daughter across the country. Now she's making it harder for me to see her this Christmas. Changing my holiday plans because she's still playing the same bull-shit games she did when we were married had me almost skipping this party tonight. Except . . . I watch the main entrance to see if Avery has arrived yet.

"Guy like you can write your own ticket," Mike continues. "I mean look at how you scored this hosting gig. How'd you enjoy working with Avery, by the way?"

His eyebrows waggle suggestively. "She's something else, huh?"

I stiffen, not much liking him or the look in his eyes.

"What do you mean?" I take my time sipping a little more of my drink, watching him over the glass.

"I mean, did you get any? We've all tried." He offers a careless shrug. "Who wouldn't try with a rack like that, but she was devoted to her fiancé. With him gone, she's been shut down. I just thought if anyone could finally tap that, it'd be you."

My teeth clench around an expletive. I know for a fact *Twofer* blows this douche's ratings out of the water. The respect of her colleagues is so important to Avery. Hearing him demean her this way sets me on edge.

"You're an asshole, you know that?" I ask, my tone deceptively calm, though my hand clamps around the glass while I imagine his little windpipe crushing under my fingers.

"So I've been told." He flashes his very-white veneers in that fake smile unsuspecting viewers fall for. "But there's no disrespect. It *has* been a year, and you know what the final stage of grief is, right?"

"Acceptance?"

"Nope." He leers over his scotch. "Horny. Somebody's gotta offer her a dick to cry on."

I'm two seconds from smashing my glass into his skull when his eyes latch onto something over my shoulder and light up.

"Damn," he mutters. "I really hope we've reached the final stage."

He's walking off before I process what he means, but it doesn't take long to figure out. Across the room, he and several other anchors and network executives are buzzing around Avery like she's a honeycomb. And I can't blame them. Her hair is pulled up, tendrils of it licking around her neck and ears. Simple gold earrings dangle and frame the curve of her cheekbones. Her makeup is dramatic, but simple, letting her sharply-drawn features speak for themselves. The slick of gold on her lips glimmers against the light copper of her skin.

And that dress.

This dress has to be inspiring erections all over the room. I can only speak for mine with any confidence, but it's pushing painfully against the flap of my suit pants.

The color, like saffron sprinkled over her firm curves, sets off her dusky complexion perfectly. Sleeveless, the dress showcases the feminine sculpture of her arms, and the neckline dips almost to her waist, the cut of it serving her breasts up beautifully. The bodice flows into a narrow skirt that paints the dress onto the flare of her hips and the tight line of her thighs. When she turns around and walks to the bar, many eyes zero in on her departure. The dress has no back, displaying a stretch of unblemished skin from neck to waist. The skirt strains across the high arc of her ass, and my fingers itch to squeeze it while I piston in and out, anchoring us together with nothing but my hands and my dick.

I take another measured sip, checking myself and allowing the smooth liquid to cool me off. I sound as bad as the other lechers in here. Mike may joke about her grief, but I've seen it up close. Even while the air sizzled with lust around us at her front door, I couldn't ignore the sadness in Avery's eyes. I won't take advantage of that. If I can help it, none of these horny sons of bitches will either.

"We do have hors d'oeuvres, you know," Sadie says from beside me. "You don't have to eat Avery."

I smile to acknowledge Sadie's comment and her presence, but I don't take my eyes off the only woman I'm interested in.

"I've seen the food." I glance down at Avery's best friend. "Far less appetizing than she is."

"You do always look at her like she's dessert." Sadie giggles. She's not usually a giggling kind of woman, so I attribute that tinkly sound to the glass of champagne. Probably not her first.

"I don't look at Avery like she's dessert." I drop the smile so she knows my intentions aren't of the short-lived, guilty pleasure variety.

"I look at her like she's the main course."

That penetrates her tipsy bubble enough to widen her eyes with surprise.

"Hmmm." She takes another sip, brows up. "Tread carefully, if that's the case. You'd be better off settling for dessert, Deck. Short and sweet."

"Do I seem like a man who settles to you?" My laugh is humorless because I'm afraid this time I might have to.

"Avery's been through a lot this year." Sadie's eyes appear suddenly slightly sober. "And she doesn't need some player making things more complicated than they already are for her."

"*Former* player," I say. "In every sense of the word."

"Would your ex-wife agree on the former?"

"What the hell does that mean?" We trade glares over her presumption.

"Meaning I know they don't take the trash out of those tunnels every night, and ballers like you scoop it up, take it home, fuck it, and don't let a wedding ring stop you."

"I never cheated on my wife." I check the anger and frustration her assumptions are burning under my collar. "If you're asking if I got ass when I was single, then let me assure you, I got ass. If you're asking if I *still* get ass, then yeah. I *still* get ass, but if I'm in a monogamous relationship, I play one-on-one. Not that it's any of your damn business."

"Avery is my damn business." She mutters under her breath what sounds like "*cabron.*"

"If you're gonna call me a motherfucker, you can do it in English." Humor relaxes my shoulders a little after the last few tense moments.

"You speak Spanish?" She doesn't look chagrined at getting caught.

"Only enough to realize I'm being insulted from time to time."

Her mouth loosens into a slight grin before she looks up at me frankly.

"Look, Avery may seem like she's having a great time." She waves her hand at the dance floor where Avery is dancing her ass off while managing to hold a Cosmopolitan. "But like the song says, blame it on the alcohol. The last thing she needs is some one-night stand holiday cheer."

"I know that." I hate the defensive note in my voice, but I resent her thinking I'm like Mike Dunlov, looking to capitalize on Avery's vulnerability.

"But do you know that today is the day?" Sadie asks softly. "That her fiancé died a year ago today?"

"Shit." I swipe a hand over my face. "I didn't know that."

I return the assessing look Sadie's giving me, and then some. Can I trust her? Can she trust me?

"What can you tell me about him?" I ask. "About his death?"

"Nothing." Sadie's mouth tips in a wry grin. "If you're serious about Avery being the . . . how'd you put it? Main course? Then that's a story she needs to tell you herself."

"Sadie!" Jerry, a cameraman I've seen on set, calls from a few feet away. "Get out here and shake what your mama gave you."

"This may take a while." Sadie laughs and hands me her glass. "'Cause Mama gave me a lot!"

She shuffles off toward the dance floor. As soon as a server passes by, I set her glass and my barely-touched Jack and Coke on the tray. The party is in full swing, but I'm already thinking about the bed upstairs in my borrowed penthouse suite. Knowing how hard today has to be for Avery, there's no way I'm leaving her at the mercy of these wolves.

Some Mariah Carey Christmas song comes on. The one from *Love Actually*. Everyone starts singing along and dancing even harder. I hate dancing. I was that guy sitting in VIP balancing a girl on each leg since I didn't really drink and definitely didn't dance. Just posted up, which is all I plan to do tonight, too. Besides, the wall gives me a great vantage point to keep an eye on Avery. If the final stage of grief is horny, I may have to protect her from herself. With Sadie off shaking what her mama gave her, it's up to me to keep Avery's virtue intact. Ironic since I've wanted in those pants for a very long time.

Another Mariah Carey Christmas song comes on.

What is *up* with Mariah Carey and the holidays?

Some other guy steps in to dance with Avery. She's good, her body moving gracefully, that dress hanging on to her curves by a literal thread. If she pops it one more inch, I think we'll have a wardrobe malfunction on our hands. Her expression is open and free like I've never seen it, but that could be because of the drink in her hand every time she dances by.

A slower song comes on, and the guy pulls Avery close, his hands slipping to her hips and his palms drifting lower. She laughs up at him and steps back, shaking her empty glass and heading to the bar.

My turn.

"Merry Christmas." I lean against the bar and block Avery's view of the rest of the room.

The smile she's been wearing since she walked through the door wavers. Her lashes drop before she looks back up at me, that fraudulent grin firmly back in place. We've seen each other on set and in meetings, but since that kiss, I've given her the space she requested.

"Not quite Christmas." She sips the drink the bartender just handed her. "Another few days."

I glance from the alcohol to her dark, glassy eyes that, up this close, are rimmed with sorrow. "What you drinking?"

"A lot." Her laugh comes loud and hollow. "I'm drinking a lot."

"I can see that." I clear my throat and lean a little closer. "You might want to ease up. Some of these guys are on the prowl tonight."

"*They're* on the prowl?" The hazy eyes turn defiant. "Maybe *I'm* on the prowl, Deck. Maybe I'm not the prey, but the hunter."

"Huntress, I think you mean."

"Hunter, huntress, whatever. I just might be prowling, so don't worry about me." She straightens from the bar and starts past me back to the dance floor. "Just stay out of my way."

I watch the steady sway of her hips as she resumes her place on the dance floor, immediately joined by Mike Dunlov. The asshole.

"Hey, homey." I proffer a hundred-dollar bill to the bartender between two fingers. "This is yours if you can water down her drinks when she comes back for more."

His eyes widen and then crinkle with a smile while he pockets the cash.

"Sure thing." He pours vodka into a cocktail shaker. "I feel for her. I do all SportsCo's parties, and she and her fiancé were great together. It's only been a year since he passed. Gotta be hard."

"Yeah," I say without offering more.

I hate discussing her like this. I've found myself in three conversations about how she's handling her grief, and none of them with her. I know she's not ready for what I'm ready for. Hell, I'm not even sure I'm ready for what I think things could be with Avery. I don't have to be in her bed tonight, but I'd love to be in her head; to know what's behind that hollow laugh and that out-of-body look. Like she's here, dancing, drinking, flirting; going through all the motions, but she's somewhere else, alone and miserable. Not really here at all.

The deejay gears the tempo down again, and Sam Smith's cover of "Have Yourself A Merry Little Christmas" comes on. Avery freezes in the middle of the dance floor, but Mike Dunlov keeps rocking, talking incessantly, barely noticing that Avery stands rigid in front of him. He misses the look of absolute devastation that twists her expression and floods her eyes. She walks off, leaving him alone wearing his confusion all over himself. I follow her path past Mike and around the corner. A few feet ahead of me, she grabs a bottle of champagne from one of the servers and steps out of sight onto the balcony.

Cold wind slaps me in the face when I join her at the rail. Noticing gooseflesh prickling the skin of her arms and back, I slip my jacket off and drape it over her shoulders. She jumps, spilling champagne down the front of her dress.

"Shit." She holds the glass and the bottle away from her body, assessing the damage.

"Sorry." I pull a cocktail napkin from my pocket and pat the wet spot on the front of her dress. "Didn't mean to startle you."

With a half-hearted grin, she watches my hands moving over the scarce material of her bodice and skirt.

"If this is some elaborate scheme to get to second base," she says. "It might actually work tonight."

My hands pause just under her breasts, and I glance from the stain on her dress to the stain on her face. The stain of sadness with a shade of inebriation.

"As much as I'd like to take you up on your offer," I say, crooking one side of my mouth even though I don't feel like smiling, and it looks like she doesn't either. "I'll take a rain check."

She narrows her eyes for a second before shrugging, setting her glass on the balcony ledge and tipping the bottle to her lips, eyes never leaving mine.

"Some other guy's lucky night then," she drawls.

I grab her wrist before she can take another sip, and the rim of the bottle is poised at her lips.

"No."

It's one word, but it covers a lot. No, she doesn't need to drink anymore. No, it's not some other motherfucker's lucky night if I have anything to say about it. And no, I won't let her drown her sorrows in champagne and meaningless sex tonight.

"No? I'm a grown-ass woman, Deck," she snaps, a shadow flitting across her face. "Grown and fancy-free."

A lone tear streaks through her flawless makeup. "God, I hate this song."

I tune into the music drifting out to us from inside.

"Have Yourself A Merry Little Christmas"? I ask.

"It was his favorite Christmas song," she whispers and clunks the champagne bottle down on the balcony ledge. "It's awful."

She squeezes her eyes closed, but more tears slip over her cheeks. I want to put my arms around her again like I did at her apartment, but she's been so unpredictable tonight, I don't know how she'll respond. I hesitate, not sure what to say. I hate it when people say stupid shit to a grieving person. I don't want to be that guy, and I'm not known for my sensitivity.

"I know this is a hard time for you."

She stares at me, sadness and uncertainty suspended between us like a rope bridge, before bringing the bottle to her lips and chugging without answering.

"Hey, hey." I urge the bottle down and away from her mouth. "That won't solve anything."

"Oh, you're so acquainted with grief, are you? That you know just what to do in these situations, huh? I'm so damn tired of being a situation. Of knowing everyone's wondering how I'm holding up, and wondering if I'm ready to date again. Wondering if I'm still . . ."

"Still what, Ave?"

She draws a deep breath and clutches the bottle to the smooth skin between her breasts displayed by the dipping neckline.

"You still on the top floor?" she demands. "Or has the network kicked you out already?"

"Nah." I draw the word out a little, buying a nanosecond to figure out where she's going with this. "I've got the penthouse for a few more days."

She nods, draws her brows together like she's processing what I've told her; like she's working out some problem. And then she says the words I would have given my first-year salary to hear the night we met, but now have no idea what to do about.

"Let's get out of here. Take me to your place."

NINE

Avery

KNOW THIS IS A MISTAKE. I'M HUDDLED IN THE CORNER OF THE ELEVATOR, my eyes fixed on the illuminated ascending numbers taking us inevitably to the top floor where Deck has been living the past few weeks. If I knew what was good for me, I would push the red emergency button; alert maintenance that there's an accident in progress right inside this elevator. But I can't. I woke up with this numbness spreading over my body like a plague. It's even frozen over my heart. I knew today would be painful; that it might hurt like a fresh wound, but nothing hurts and nothing feels good. Not the deceptively innocuous champagne bubbles zipping through my bloodstream. Not the many guys I danced with tonight or the secret touches they stole while we moved to the music. Nothing has made me feel all day.

Except him.

Call it lust. Animal attraction. Whatever it is, I felt it like a shot of adrenaline as soon as I saw Decker tonight. I study him from under surreptitious lashes, roving my eyes over silky hair the color of nutmeg brushed with honey. The slightest curl of it at his nape softens the hard line of his neck. His brandy-flavored eyes watch the climbing numbers, the bold nose and thick brows and wide, mobile mouth harmonizing his features into handsome. I study the impressive width of his shoulders and the bulge of his arms straining against the dress shirt. His jacket around my shoulders douses me in his scent and his warmth. I discretely snuggle deeper into its embrace, even though the arms hang limp and empty at my sides.

Yes, he makes me feel something. I want it to be as simple as lust; as the sad, horny girl who woke up with her dead fiancé on her mind and her hand between her legs, but it's not that simple. I've always known with Decker it wouldn't be.

"I don't think . . ." I struggle to wrangle my thoughts set on a wild goose chase by the alcohol I've consumed. "I'm not sure this is a good idea."

He looks at me sharply just as the doors open to his floor. We consider each other, neither making a move. The doors start closing and he catches them with one long arm.

"Come on." He tilts his head toward the landing beyond the elevator doors. "At least let me get some coffee in you. Sober you up and save you from bad decisions you'll regret tomorrow."

He thinks the bad decisions are back at the party with idiots like Mike Dunlov. No, the bad decisions are behind his closed doors, but I find myself half-stumbling after him to the penthouse. As soon as we're inside, I lean my palm onto the wall for balance and take off my stilettos. I lose another four inches, and now have to tip my head farther back to see his face.

"You're tall." I want to retract the obvious statement to a basketball player as soon as it trips past my liquor-loosened lips. Humor flits through his eyes briefly before concern swipes it away.

"Comes with the territory." He walks toward the small, neat kitchen. "Come on. Coffee."

I very carefully climb onto the leather stool at the counter, looping my bare feet on the slats. Decker makes even a simple task like making coffee look tantalizing. The play of muscles under his thin white shirt when he reaches for a mug. The efficiency of his big hands, quick and deft in the mundane preparations. There's a rugged grace to him; like rough metal that's been polished and chiseled until it gleams.

"You're beautiful," I blurt, causing him to stop what he's doing and stare at me.

I really *am* drunk. I'd never say that sober.

"Wow, you really *are* drunk." He echoes my thoughts, laughs and shakes his head, sliding the coffee across the marble counter top. "Drink this and I'm sure I'll be less beautiful soon."

I hope so because if he keeps looking like that, I can't be held responsible.

And isn't that what I want? For one night not to feel responsible? Not to feel guilty or condemned? Ashamed of my part in Will's irreversible decision? All night I've wanted to feel something, and in this moment, I feel everything. Like a wall dropped and every painful thought and emotion rushed in before I could get my guard back up.

"It's today," I speak into the quiet filled with only the hum of appliances.

"What's today?" Decker leans his elbows on the counter, gathering both huge fists under his chin and watching me closely, waiting for more.

I think he already knows. All night it felt like everyone knew I was desperate to forget the significance of this day.

"Um . . . a year ago today, Will died." I run a fingernail over the silky material stretching across my thighs.

"I'm sorry, Avery." Sincerity lays heavy in the dark eyes, unlit by his usual good humor.

"Did you know it was suicide?" The words cut my tongue like a razor. "That he took his own life? Right in our apartment."

"I didn't know. Did you . . ." His compassion reshapes to horror. "Did you find him, Avery?"

The horrible tableau plays out across my mind again like it has countless times before.

"Yeah." My whisper breaks. "I found him, but I was too late."

Despite the warmth of his jacket around me, I shiver like I'm back there; like the premonition that slid over me when I entered our apartment that night is revisiting my skin and reminiscing with my bones.

"Shit, Ave." Decker crosses around the counter to me, his taut stomach hitting my bent knees while I sit on the stool. "I'm so sorry."

"He was . . . he was . . ." My teeth rattle, shock shaking me like I'm standing in that bathroom again. "In the water. In our bathtub with so much blood."

Deck pulls me closer by the shoulders while tears course over my cheeks and dampen the fine cotton of his shirt. I can't catch my breath. Weeping quakes my body with the stupid tears I promised myself I wouldn't shed today. I was so determined to forget all of this tonight, and here I am, a sloppy mess all over Mack Decker. His wide, warm palms roll over my arms when his jacket falls from my shoulders and hits the thick pile carpet. He rests his hands at the curve of my neck and shoulder when my tears finally subside, his thumbs under my chin, lifting, forcing my eyes to meet his.

"Hey, you okay?" he asks softly.

I concentrate all my senses, all my focus on where his hands have been. My arms are warm from his touch. The sensitive skin of my neck tingles where his thumbs caress. The faint smell of alcohol and his expensive cologne flares my nostrils. My heart slams into my ribs like I've run and leapt and landed. Wordlessly, I scoot forward on the stool, widening my legs until he's between them, bracketed by my knees. The bold action forces the dress up to the juncture of my thighs, offering a glimpse of my black panties. His eyes drop between my legs and snap up to my face. He tries to step back, hands falling away and jaw ticking, but I latch onto one leanly muscled arm.

"Don't." I scoot forward more until I'm barely on the stool. "Please don't leave me like this, Deck."

"I'm not leaving you, Avery. I . . ." He gives a decisive shake of his head. "You're not in a good place tonight and I won't take advantage of that. I want to help you, not . . ."

His words trail away and his eyes are distracted, following a path along my collarbone, between my breasts, over my stomach and between my legs. I spread my thighs another inch, showing him what he's wanted for a long time and inviting him to take it tonight.

He licks his bottom lip, a fascinating swipe of his tongue that I lean forward and mimic with my own. His pleasured groan vibrates against my mouth, but he pulls back, drawing in a deep breath and shaking his head again.

"Ave, I—"

I grip him by the neck and lick the seam of his lips. His jaw drops on a gasp, and I push my tongue in, exploring the warm, silky interior of his mouth. My hands venture between us, finding him lengthened, hardened. When I squeeze, he growls into our kiss. His hands, which have remained in deliberate discipline at his sides, encompass my waist. They're so big his fingers almost meet at my back and his thumbs rest under my breasts. My nipples tauten in proximity to his touch.

"You're playing with fire here." His voice emerges rough as Brillo.

"I know exactly," I say, my voice husky while my hand pushes up and down over his dick. "what I'm playing with."

"Avery, we should—"

"Make me feel," I cut in, steadily pumping him through his pants. "You want to help, then make me feel."

Tears gather at the edges of my eyes, trickling unchecked over my face and into the corners of my mouth.

"Make me feel something other than pain, Deck." I meet his eyes, and they reflect my sorrow back to me. He groans when my hand persists.

"Promise me," he finally says, searching my face. "Promise me you won't regret this tomorrow."

A dissonant laugh flows out of me, misplaced in the grief and lust permeating the room around us.

"I can't promise you I won't regret this tomorrow." I stare back at him, not hiding my pain or my passion or my confusion or my need. "I can only promise that I want it like hell tonight."

TEN

Decker

AVERY'S WORDS, EVEN MORE THAN HER HAND, GRAB ME BY THE BALLS. The sight of her arrests my heart in my chest. I've wanted this woman for a long time, but knew it would probably never happen. Here she is offering herself to me on a very unexpected platter, and I'm not sure I can do anything about it. Because after all this time, I'll be damned if I'm settling for one night with her; some drunken memory she relegates to the back of a closet and never considers repeating.

"Deck, I just want to feel good." Her lips tremble when she presses them to mine again. "Make me feel. Make me come."

"Shit," I hiss at her brazen request. "Avery, I can't. Any night but tonight. I can't."

Surprise and hurt mingle in her dark eyes, calcifying into determination. She hops off the stool and stands, allowing no space between us so I feel the heavy heave of her breasts against my chest.

"Okay." She looks up at me, her mouth a stiff line set in delicate bones. "Maybe Mike can—"

"The hell Mike."

My hands clamp around her waist, stopping her from walking to the door. I swallow the last of my hesitation. She doesn't know if she'll regret this tomorrow. I'm almost certain I will, but I lose the fight with my will, with hers, and lift her back onto the stool. She wants to feel? She wants to come? Never looking away from her face, I drop to my knees and press her open. She doesn't resist. Her legs relax, stopping where I want them. I rub my stubbled chin and cheek along the sensitive skin inside her thighs, rewarded by the gasps above my head. The closer I get to my goal, the harder it is to breathe. The smell of her reaches my nose, unhinging my restraint. I tighten my hands around her thighs, forcing myself to go slow; to be gentle. I lift her legs over my shoulders, dragging her ass to the very edge of the stool to mouth her through the black panties. They're already damp, and her flavor seeps onto my tongue, so sweet I can't help but remember Sadie saying Avery could be my dessert.

"Oh, my God, Deck." Her words are needy and breathless.

I don't look up, too absorbed in the taste of her, even through silk. So potent. I nudge the panties aside with my nose, licking up her seam. She's wet and hot and tangy on my lips. I delve into her slickness, seeking out the crown jewel tucked inside, that cluster of nerves. I suck hard, and she bucks into my mouth. The steady interplay of tongue, lips and teeth at the intersection of her body and my mouth has her hips jerking and her hand clawing my hair. Her hips roll in tandem with me, and I glance up long enough to watch her inhibitions fall away. Her head drops back, the satin skin of her throat stretched and taut with pleasure.

"Deck, I'm gonna . . . oh God."

I slip two fingers inside, still sucking and licking while both her hands grip my head; while she commands me like a queen in her inner court. Her legs quake against me and her body tightens around my fingers convulsively as she comes. She rides it out over my mouth, taking anything I might not be giving her. Except I'm giving her everything, and she doesn't even know it.

When her body goes still, and the only sound in the room is our labored breathing, I slide away from her. That's as far as I'll allow myself to go. She wanted to feel. She wanted to come. I've done that for her, but I have to get her out of here.

"Don't, Deck." Her lipstick is smeared and her lips are swollen from our kiss. "Don't stop."

Her hips start rocking again like her pussy is remembering what I feel like; like she's seeking something. Seeking me. The panties still pushed aside, showing me how needy and creamy she is between her thighs. I'm shaking my head, a definite denial, but when she slides the shoulders of her dress away, her breasts are naked and perfect. Most nipples are small tight buds, but Avery's are lengthened and plump and plum-colored, resting at the tips of her breasts like heavy fruit on a vine. I want to drink. I'm already dizzy with the taste of her, but the sight of her unravels my convictions until they are shredded into ribbons at our feet. She stands, pushing at the skirt, sliding it over her hips and legs, a puddle of silk at her bare feet. She's only in the black panties, but even those she persuades down her body until she's naked for me.

She traces the tip of her finger over my eyebrows, down my nose, skims my lips, cups my jaw.

"You really are beautiful," she whispers, her eyes following the path her finger took. "Give me tonight, Deck."

I got nothing left. Any resistance melts under the awe in her eyes as she runs them over my face, as her look probes beneath my clothes. I want to show her. I want her to be as enamored with my body as I am with hers. I stand up, towering over her. I pull her bare back to my chest and walk us to the bedroom, all the way, cupping her breasts, pinching her nipples, caressing her stomach, pressing my hard-on into her ass, so that by the time we reach my bedroom, her breaths are ragged, her fingers trembling when she unbuttons my shirt. I stand perfectly still, watching her eyes glaze over with every portion of me she reveals. She fumbles with my belt, but I don't intervene, enjoying the clumsy brush of her fingers against my stomach. She opens my zipper, deliberately skimming a knuckle over me through my briefs, making my breath catch and cut in my chest. A little grin quirks one corner of her mouth when she sees my reaction. She pushes the shirt off my shoulders, leaning forward to suck my nipples.

"God, Ave." My fingers lace into the hair neatly gathered up, dislodging pins so it spills around her shoulders.

She shoves my pants down, following their path to my feet, settling onto her knees. Her velvety brown eyes peer up at me, hot and hungry, as she tugs my underwear over my legs, her hands tracing the muscles of my thighs and calves.

"Oh, my God." She stares at my dick, elongated and thick, bobbing at the entrance of her lips. "I'm not sure I can take it all."

"Won't know till you try." I line up with her mouth. "Open."

Obediently, her full lips part, and I push in, groaning every inch of the way.

"Mmmmmm." She clumps her eyebrows together, and for a moment I think it's too much; that it's discomfort tightening her expression. Then she lowers her jaw, taking me deeper into the tight channel of her throat.

"Mmmmmm," she spreads her hands over my ass, gripping as much of me as she can. She presses in closer, rubbing her breasts over my legs in sync with her mouth, sharpening her nipples against me, using me. It's turning me on even more.

"Shit, you give good head," I mumble, barely able to form coherent words. I bite my bottom lip until it throbs, a counter to the bliss happening below my waist.

She adds her hand to the equation, cupping my balls, pulling her mouth from the root all the way to the tip and insinuating her tongue into the tiny opening.

"Sweet mother of . . ." I grip her jaw, holding her at just the perfect angle, and fuck her mouth relentlessly, my hips a merciless cadence while tears streak over her face. I don't know if the tears are sadness, or if she's choking on my dick, but she won't let me go. Her fingers lock so tight on my ass, her nails dig into the muscles.

I will burst soon, and it will be inside of her. I carefully pull back and skim my palms over the fragile framework of her collarbone and shoulders, spreading my hands open, just whispering the palms over her nipples again and again. Her mouth drops open, lashes fall to kiss her cheeks and she leans back onto her heels, pressing her arms behind her, the muscles in her legs strained, palms to the floor so she's offering herself to me. I keep working in tight circles over her breasts, and her hips jerk in time with my pace.

I lift her gently onto the bed behind us and spread her out, taking myself in my hand and pumping, making her wait. Making her watch. She moves her legs restlessly, looking for relief.

"Come on, Deck." She licks her lips, eyes fixed on my dick.

I straddle her hips with my knees, letting my cock rub between her legs in tantalizing swipes.

"Give it to me." She reaches for it, trying to line us up.

"You'll get it when I'm ready, Ave." My voice is hoarse and scratchy, and I want to be buried inside her, but draw it out for us both.

I take one nipple between my lips, varying the suction from gentle and barely there, to rough and aggressive. All the while pinching the other and rolling the nipple between my fingers. I transfer my mouth to the other breast and slide my hand, palm flat against her belly, between her legs.

She jerks when I peel back the lips and rub my fingertip over her clit in a swift rhythm. It plumps and tightens.

"Damn, you're wet," I groan, seduced by the sloppy sounds her pussy makes when I finger fuck her.

"I need it to be now, Deck," she pants, stretching her legs wide and tugging at my hips. Positioning me.

"Okay. Just one more taste." I want her juices on my tongue when I enter her for the first time.

"No," she growls, her eyes narrow and her face tight with passion. "Now."

I can't help but chuckle because she looks so fierce; so much like the girl who put me in my place at my locker. So much like the driven, ambitious, commanding woman I've come to admire from a distance over the last few years, even more up close the last few weeks.

"Now, you said?" With no more warning, I thrust inside, and we share a gasp at the perfect fit. I know I'm big and she's tight as hell, but it feels perfect to me.

"You all right?" I crush the urge to slam into her, waiting for her to indicate it's okay to move. "Are you—"

"If you don't come on and fuck me, Mack Decker," she rasps, eyes half-mast and hands clenched around my ass.

My dick twitches inside of her at the coarse words, and she grins, locking her ankles behind my back. She better lock 'em. She has no idea how hard she's about to get fucked. I hitch an arm under her knee and grind in so deep my balls get wet.

Her eyes go wide, and her body moves up the bed with the first few thrusts. I pump into her at full force, rocking the headboard into the wall, making the mattress moan.

"Oh my God." One of her hands leaves my ass and grips the sheet at her side. "This is . . . oh my God."

I push her knees to her shoulders, folding her back, appreciating how pliable her body is under my hands. I glance down to watch myself enter and withdraw, watch the evidence of how much she wants me on my dick.

On my dick. Fuck.

"Condom." I pull out, and her face crumples.

"No, don't stop."

"Let me get this on." I reach into the bedside table, wrap it up in record speed, and get back in there, pulling her legs over my shoulders.

"Oh, yes." She links her fingers behind my neck and tosses her head on the pillow. She clenches around me, stiffens with wave after wave of her orgasm.

"I feel so much." She stretches her neck back, lifting slightly off the pillow. Tears slide over her cheeks. "Oh, my God. It feels amazing."

Her eyes meet mine in the dim light, and she shows me every-thing. The things she hasn't told me, the secrets that torture her. I may not have the words yet, but the feeling, the hurt shadows her pleasure and she tells me everything. The intimacy of it pushes me over, and I'm exploding, throwing my head back, gripping her hips, my body reduced to urges and instincts and thrusts and moans until I finish, sinking my teeth into the tender curve of her neck.

I roll onto my back, keeping her connected to me, staying in-side of her, our bellies kissing. Her legs fall limply on either side of my hips. She pushes up onto her elbows to study me, tears spilling unapologetically down her face. Her mouth trembles, works around sounds for a few seconds before she speaks.

"You made me feel," she whispers. "Damn you."

And then she collapses onto my chest and weeps.

ELEVEN

Avery

"**H**E LEFT A NOTE."

The confession slips seamlessly into the intimacy our bodies, maybe even our hearts, made in this bed. In the darkness of this room only brightened by the skyline twinkling beyond the window.

"What?" Deck adjusts me in the crook of his shoulder, kissing my temple and pushing my hair aside to nuzzle into my neck, too. "What'd you say, Ave?"

He sounds sleepy. We just finished round two, and I must say I've never been fucked like that in my life. It was . . . possession and dominance and tenderness and ferocity taking turns, all sides of him sharing me. I love the way he arranges me exactly how he wants, pushes my legs back just so. Tips my ass up to the desired angle. Spreads me to his specifications. And then fucks me like a train.

The man fucks like a train.

And I've been railroaded; possibly ruined for everyone else. If I had known there were men out there, fucking like that, I'd have a lot more notches on my bedpost in my quest to find them.

"Ave?" he asks again, reminding me of what I want to tell him, as much as I would love to stay distracted thinking of what we just did . . . twice. For the first time, I want to tell someone other than my therapist the secret I've been wearing like an albatross around my neck for the last year.

"He, um . . . Will, my fiancé. He left a note."

Deck shifts, carefully pulling his shoulder from under my head so he can lie on his side. So he can see my face while he waits for me to go on. I punish my lip trapped between my teeth.

"It was in the bathroom with my ring."

In the sliver of silence following my last words, I know he's mentally assembling the pieces of this puzzle before he asks his next question.

"You weren't wearing your ring?"

The question comes low and soft, a sympathetic query. Not a threat or an accusation or any of the things I've told myself I deserve.

"No, I had taken it off a few days before." I try to swallow, but can't past the scalding, swollen walls of my throat. "I . . . I . . . God, I . . ."

My breaths come in choppy heaves. I clutch the sheet to my naked breasts to keep my hands from shaking.

"Hey, hey." Decker cups my jaw in one big hand, brushing his thumb over the tears trickling down my cheek. "Baby, it's okay. Take your time."

It's been so long since a man called me "baby." Since I shared any intimacy with another person. Long before Will and I ended, our sex life dried up. The casual affection of intimate touches, naked skin, bared souls and endearments had long departed.

"I broke our engagement off a few days before he killed himself." The admission storms past my lips as if the words know this is their last chance; know that if they don't escape now I won't ever let them out.

Decker scoots down until his forehead lines up with mine, the height difference so great my feet stop at his knees under the cover.

"I'm so sorry." He dusts kisses over my wet cheeks, spearing his long fingers into my hair. "I can't even imagine. Tell me."

I stare through the dim light, searching his face for judgment, but it's not there; just a patient, waiting compassion. It gives me courage to go on.

"We had been over for a long time, I think." I squeeze my eyes tightly closed. "He suffered from depression. His medication made it so much better, but he didn't like to take it. Sometimes he wouldn't take it, and he wouldn't take care of himself. He'd lose friends. His work would go bad."

I lick at the bitter smile festering on my lips.

"We would go bad."

I shrug and shiver, pulling the sheet tighter around me. "I would say he wasn't trying hard enough. He would say I didn't understand. We'd . . . fight. We stopped . . ."

My voice dies in the dark. I dip my head to hide my face, ashamed to hear my part in this tragedy spoken aloud.

"You stopped what, Ave?" Deck probes gently, kissing my forehead and encouraging me to go on. "You can tell me."

"We stopped . . ." I glance up at him through a dampened veil of eyelashes. "We stopped making love. We were like roommates, miserable more often than not, but determined to keep trying. I loved him. I did, but I'm not sure for the last year or so that I was *in* love with him."

My harsh laugh puffs across our lips, just inches apart.

"Hell, he probably wasn't in love with me either there at the end," I say. "He went on a business trip and he cheated."

Deck's hard body goes still, and his thumb caresses under my chin, urging my eyes up to meet his.

"He was a fool," Deck says. "Not to speak ill of the dead, but anyone who isn't satisfied with you is a fool."

"No, I was a shrew." I wince, replaying some of our arguments. "We both wanted it to work so badly. We loved who we were in the beginning, but we weren't those people anymore. At least not to each other."

I always knew Will had . . . spells. Seasons when he would withdraw because life felt too hard, and nothing, not even our closeness, could pull him out. I didn't realize how bad it was until last year, and even then, I never imagined he'd harm himself. He stopped going to work. Stopped eating and showering regularly. Stopped making love to me. Stopped everything that made him happy. Stopped everything that made him . . . Will. He stopped everything that made us . . . us, and it broke my heart. Long before anonymous out-of-town hook up ho, my heart had been broken in minutes and hours and over days. We drifted out of love, into heartbreak, and settled into a terrible indifference. We were unrecognizable, and I didn't know if it would have happened eventually anyway, or if his depression, the wall it erected between us, forced us to it.

"So, what happened?" Decker prompts.

"When he told me he'd cheated, I. . ." I want to cover my ears against the memory of our raised voices; of our hurtful words. "I gave him his ring back. I told him it was over and went to a hotel."

Guilt assails me, fresh and wrenching. My heartbeat accelerates and my pulse pounds in my ears.

"That was the last time I saw him alive." I struggle to get the words out. "How could I do that, Deck? I knew he was depressed, was struggling, but I never thought he'd do something like that."

"Not your fault, Ave." He squeezes my chin between his fingers firmly. "Don't do that to yourself."

Doing that to myself has become a habit I'm not sure I can break. Blaming myself for what happened.

"When I broke it off, he thought I would reconsider, and asked that we not tell our friends and family yet so no one knew that just days before, I'd . . ."

Abandoned him. Left him on his own. Left him to die.

The details of that night overtake what I see, what I hear, hurling me back into that cold bathroom. All the sounds and images and horrors flood my memory. I'd gone to the apartment to tell him I was sure; that we should go ahead and tell everyone it was over. Not just because of him cheating, but because we weren't working anymore and hadn't for a long time. As soon as I let myself into the apartment, I'd heard the music drifting from the back to the entrance.

Have yourself a merry little Christmas
Let your heart be light
From now on your troubles will be out of sight

The closer I'd gotten to the bathroom, the louder the music became and the more I was sure something was wrong. The air trembled with it. Each lyric ached with the pain I'd seen in Will for years, ebbing, flowing, sometimes less, sometimes more—always there, but finally too much.

"He was in the tub," I whisper, my eyes unfocused on the room I'm in now, but seeing that other room; seeing Will in water turned scarlet with his blood. Seeing the deep lines sliced in his wrists, perpendicular to his pain; intersecting with the misery I'd seen in his eyes for months, but been helpless to soothe. I hadn't known his despair went that deep.

I still see that note, my name scrawled in Will's loopy penmanship. I still see the ring I had returned to him there on the counter.

"Avery, I tried," I say, my mouth trembling, an unsteady messenger for Will's last words. "That's all the note said. That he tried."

Was it an apology? For cheating? For giving up? Was it a condemnation of me, for underestimating his despair? For pushing too hard? For wanting too much? Always more from him, or for him? The questions make well-worn laps in my mind, round and round, dizzying me with the finality of Will's one-sided farewell.

The song. The tub. The blood. The ring. The note.

Second after painful second, I manage to drag myself out, like I've had to do so many times since that night. I focus on Decker, pleading for him to understand, or maybe to help me understand.

"Sometimes I'd say he wasn't trying because that's all I know how to do," I say. "I've spent my whole life *trying*. Achieving. Making things happen for myself, and on some level, I didn't understand that it wasn't that easy for him. That it wasn't about trying. It was deeper than that. For him it was harder than that. Maybe he was trying until he just couldn't try anymore. And I saw that too late, Deck, and now he's gone."

My shoulders shake with the emotion I've been hiding from for a year.

"When I saw the note, it had my name on it. No one else's." I shrug helplessly. "There was no message for anyone else, so I kept it to myself."

My laugh comes out hollow, barely a laugh at all.

"And if I'm honest, I didn't want anyone to know. To blame me like I blamed myself." I swipe trembling fingers over my wet cheeks. "God, I didn't want his mother to blame me like I blame myself. For her to think he did that because of me."

The words slip-slide on my tears, barely discernible, but Deck understands. He pulls me close, one hand stroking at the small of my back and one hand cupping my face as he kisses the wetness on my cheeks.

"Listen to me." His voice falls soft and firm over my hiccupping. "I don't know what you could have done differently in your relationship. When a relationship fails, we look backward with much more perspective than when we're in it. Believe me. I learned that after my divorce."

I sniff and nod against his chest for him to go on.

"And replaying our arguments and rehearsing our mistakes won't change how we handled things," he says. "But in a situation like that, you aren't responsible for someone making that decision. Our lives are just that."

He dips his head to catch and hold my eyes with his.

"Ours." He frowns, pressing his lips together over a sigh. "You remember that *Sports Illustrated* party a couple years ago?"

"Yeah."

We hadn't spoken, but I remember that lightning strike of seeing Deck again after so long. How my palms went sweaty and my heart went haywire and my stomach went all fluttery. I had seen him from time to time over the years from a distance, but that night, he'd been so close. Closer than he had been for a long time, and as much as I made sure nobody knew, it affected me. *He* affected me.

"I wanted your fiancé out of the way." His voice is gruff, prompting me to pull back just enough to see his face. "And I didn't care that I was there with Tara. I didn't care that you were with him. I'd wanted you for years, since the first time I saw you, and I resented him touching you. Resented his ring on your finger. I resented him having you when I never got my chance."

He pauses, a deep swallow bobbing his Adam's apple.

"I thought about that when I heard he had died," Decker says. "I felt guilty for even wishing him out of the way."

"But you didn't . . ." I pause to sort my thoughts and find the right words. "You had nothing to feel guilty about. Your desire for me didn't kill Will. He did that."

"Exactly, Avery." He brushes my hair back from my face. "Exactly."

His words sink in and I try to put myself in that place where I'm absolved of guilt. I can't quite do it yet. I know he's right theoretically, but that night I found Will wasn't theoretical. It *happened* to me, and I haven't gone a day without seeing him that way. Without asking if he was there because of me.

"I can't imagine how much pain Will was in to do something like that," Decker continues. "I assume it's something he wrestled with at other points in his life."

"All through college." I pause, before sharing another thing I haven't even told Sadie yet. "His mother actually told me his first attempt was in high school, and then again in college. I had no idea."

I shake my head, overwhelmed with how much I missed. "How did I live with him, share my life with him, wear his ring, plan our future and not know he'd tried to take his own life? Twice?"

"How would you have known if he didn't tell you?" Decker asks. "We hide in the open. We cover our scars so we can move on. Sometimes we hide because we're ashamed. Because we're afraid people won't accept us or love us or understand. No matter the reason, you didn't know. But even if you did, would you have stayed in a broken relationship for the rest of your life from fear that he would do something like this? These were demons he'd wrestled with before he even knew you, Avery. You can't take responsibility for his life, for his decision. You couldn't do it while he was alive, and you can't do it now that he's gone."

My therapist has said these things to me. I've replayed them to myself on days when I thought the guilt, the weight of his death would drive me mad. But there's a ring of truth when Decker says it that I haven't allowed myself to hear before. Maybe I thought I was letting myself off easy. In situations like this, you need someone to blame, and it feels wrong to blame Will. If I allow myself to place the responsibility with him for even a second, I become furious. I get livid with him for leaving me and his mother and his friends who care about him. Who love him and miss him and will live the rest of their lives asking the same questions I do.

Why?

How could you?

What didn't I do?

Could I have been enough to keep you here?

I want to throw things at the wall and I want to punch him in the face. More than anything, I want to rewind to an illuminating moment when I could have made a difference. I replay our years together over and over, watching from an objective distance, searching for that second when I could have looked in his eyes, seen how truly miserable he was with this life, and fixed it.

And maybe that's the problem. I've accomplished all my goals and created the destiny I envisioned for myself. A woman accomplishing what I have in sports and television is rare, much less a woman of color. I rose above expectations and limitations at every turn. I defied the odds. Every hurdle, I've jumped. Every problem, I've fixed. But I could never solve Will.

If you can't come through when it's life or death, when it counts, then what good are you?

I finally drift off to sleep in the rare comfort of someone else's arms and realize that is the question that's been haunting me. I may find no peace until I have an answer.

TWELVE

Decker

'M MAKING FRENCH TOAST WHEN SHE ENTERS THE KITCHEN THE NEXT morning.

She's not exactly shy, but she has trouble meeting my eyes. I hope it's just morning-after awkwardness, not regret. Last night was the best sex of my life. One of the best nights of my life period, even though there were tears and pain and it was hard.

It was *her*.

It was my chance to unwind the labyrinth that has been Avery all these years. To understand her and get a glimpse of what's beneath all that control. It's beautiful. So beautiful that now I'm addicted to her honesty and her vulnerability and her boldness and her brand of brokenness. If last night was my only hit, she's a high I might chase the rest of my life.

"Morning." I glance up from the toast sizzling in the pan.

"Morning." She toys with the belt of my silk robe she's wearing. The hem trails the floor behind her because there's more material than her much shorter body knows what to do with. It still looks really good on her, gaping in front, hinting at two high, perfectly round breasts and copper-toned skin stretched over a taut plane of feminine muscle in her stomach. Her hair, tousled around her shoulders, rests dark against the maroon-colored silk. She runs a self-conscious hand over the tangled strands, combing her fingers through and pushing them behind her ear.

"You look beautiful," I reassure her.

Her fingers freeze in the process of setting her hair to whatever rights she's attempting. She climbs up onto the high stool, leaning her elbows on the counter.

"Breakfast?" she asks unnecessarily.

I turn the toast with a laugh. "Looks that way."

She grimaces over my answer before surrendering a grateful smile when I pass her a cup of coffee.

"Sorry it's not your cold brew."

"It's fine." She takes a long sip. "Oh, God. Thank you."

She clears her throat, shifting a little uneasily on the stool.

"And thanks for the ibuprofen you left." She rims the lip of the mug with her finger, not looking up. "That was very thoughtful."

"You had a good bit to drink last night." I turn off the toast and start scrambling eggs in a second pan. "Thought you might be a little hungover."

A wicked smile starts in her eyes and then creeps its way to her lips.

"It's not my head that's sore."

I pause in the preparations, processing what she is saying. My laugh bounces off the kitchen walls and I walk over to her, notching my hips between her knees. My hands stroke her back through the silk. She's soft and warm and smells fresh.

"You showered?" I whisper kisses behind her ear.

"Yeah." Her answer is breathy. "Hope that's okay."

"I only hate that I missed it," I rasp at the fragrant, silky skin of her neck where my teeth marked her. "Sorry about this."

"My neck isn't sore either." She laughs, a liberated sound I want her to keep making.

"Oh." My hand wanders over her nipple and it beads under the silk. "Here?"

The slightest hitch of her breath is the only indication she's feeling this.

"No, not there."

"Hmmm." I pucker my eyebrows into a frown. "I'm running out of options."

I step deeper into the vee of her thighs until the robe splits and falls away, baring the toned length of her legs.

"Maybe it's here." I run one exploring finger from her calf, over her knee and inside her thigh, just shy of her pussy.

"You are getting so close," she says, eyes not leaving my face.

I slide a finger along either side of her clit, trapping it between the digits and then stroking it with my thumb.

"Shit," she mutters, her hips moving in the rhythm my fingers set. "That's it. Right there. Not a hangover. A fuckover."

I chuckle and stop my fingers, move my hand away.

"Oh, I'm sorry. If you're sore, maybe I shouldn't—"

"You should," she cuts in, returning my hand to her center. "Believe me you should."

And while our breakfast gets cold, I do.

Stretched out naked on my pillows, Avery licks sticky vestiges of syrup from her fingers, an empty plate in her lap and a sheet haphazardly covering her.

"That was good," she says, purring like a contented cat.

"Breakfast or . . ." I let my words trail off and I glance at the well-used bed where she writhed under me not too long ago.

"Both. Breakfast. Last night. This morning. All of it." She bites into the grin that graces her kiss-swollen lips until it fades with the careful look she angles up at me. "Thank you for everything. It was perfect."

We spent last night together, and half of today since breakfast became brunch the more we kissed and touched. And fucked.

Man, did we fuck.

And after just a day having her, it has been more intimate and more perfect than anything I experienced in years of marriage to Tara.

So the finality in Avery's voice wears on my nerves.

"You sound really grateful." I leave the bed, pulling on a pair of gray sweats from the floor and tying them at the waist. "What? You gonna send me a fruit basket or some shit?"

I meet her eyes head on, silently challenging her to tell me she regrets last night, this morning. That we won't pursue more. That it . . . *that we* . . . won't happen again.

"Deck" she starts softly, staring at her fingers toying with the sheets bunched at her waist. "We talked about this, about—"

"That was before," I butt in. "Before everything happened. Before we made love and we talked and we . . ."

I claw frustrated fingers through my hair. "Dammit, Ave, that was before and you know it."

"Nothing's changed." She scoots up to sit straighter against the headboard, gathering the sheet around her like forgotten armor. "I'm still as emotionally unavailable as I was at that party last night."

"Liar." The one word blasts into the chilling air separating us. "You were more available to me last night than any woman I've ever been with."

"I'm not talking about sexually, Deck."

"Neither the hell am I, *Avery*."

We glare at one another, our breath coming quicker with our mutual frustration. It's not totally unexpected, her withdrawal, but I thought I would have a little more time to convince her that we should try.

"I'm moving to California," I say abruptly. Her eyes widen before she catches the reaction and controls it.

"Oh, I thought . . ." She stops the nervous tugging of the sheets. "Oh."

"I told you my ex moved there. She keeps making it harder for me to see Kiera." I sigh wearily and scrub a hand over my face. "She's just pissed because she didn't get more out of the divorce."

"They say it's cheaper to keep her," Avery says with a cynical twist of her lips.

"Then 'they' don't have my lawyer or my pre-nup." We share a smile that comes a little easier to us both. "At the last minute, she pulled some crap so I have to go to LA to see my baby girl for Christmas, when she was supposed to come here for two weeks."

"I'm sorry, Deck."

"Yeah. So am I. It'll just be simpler for me to live out there." I hesitate for a moment before sitting on the edge of the bed, within touching distance if she decides to touch me. "I've been offered a front office position with that new expansion team the San Diego Waves. President of Basketball Operations, with the possibility of partial ownership eventually."

Ever the journalist, curiosity and questions stack up in Avery's wide eyes.

"And we *are* off the record, by the way," I remind her. "This isn't public yet."

"All right, all right. I get it." She pulls her legs up to her chest, resting her chin on sheet-covered knees. "Congratulations."

"Thanks. It works for me personally, so I can be closer to my daughter, and professionally because it's the kind of opportunity I've wanted, but didn't think I'd get for at least another five years."

"That's great, Deck." Her face has become the mask she showed me when we first started hosting her show together three weeks ago. "I'm happy for you."

"I don't want you to be happy for me, Avery. I want you to tell me that what we had the last twenty-four hours is enough to build on. That when I go away, we can try to build more."

"You saw me last night." Her mouth is the only thing wavering in her obstinate expression. "You know I'm a mess."

"We're all a mess." I scoot closer, palm her jaw and press my forehead to hers. "We'll figure it out."

She shakes her head against mine, not breaking the contact between our skin.

"There are some things I need to figure out on my own. Questions not just about Will, but about myself that I need to answer." She mirrors my touch, her hand cupping my jaw. "As much as I enjoyed last night, as much as I . . ."

She swallows, shutting her eyes.

"Deck, deep down you know I'm not ready."

I glance up to find her cheeks wet again, tears leaking from under her closed eyelids. I want to deny it. As much as I want to convince her that she is ready; that I'll make her ready, or be ready enough for both of us, I know it doesn't work that way. I still hear her sobs and feel her shaking in my arms, recounting the horror of finding Will in their apartment. I still hear her agony over his last words to her.

"Okay. I accept that you're not ready. I have to go to California, and I know you have to stay here in New York."

I dip my head to kiss her, coaxing her lips open for a languorous dueling of tongues that quickly ignites fire in me. In Avery, too, if her nails digging into my back are any indication.

I give her hair a gentle tug until she's looking deeply, directly into my eyes.

"The time may not be right, but we *feel* right, Ave. Tell me you see how right we feel together."

Her nod is the only answer she offers, sniffing at the fresh tears I know aren't all for Will. Aren't all for her. I know that some of them are for me. I bend to kiss her cheeks, darting my tongue out to gather the salt of her tears.

"Hey, look at me." I gently angle her face up so we have no choice but to see one another. "Promise me that when you have the answers you're looking for, that when you're ready, you'll find me."

She leans deeper into me, uncaring that the sheet drops, baring her stubble-burned breasts. She takes my mouth in a kiss that is part consolation, part declaration. She eases away, licking her lips like she can taste me there.

"That's a promise I plan to keep."

THIRTEEN

Avery

"**A**RE YOU SURE ABOUT THIS, AVERY?"

I ease into my cashmere coat and turn to face my mother.

"Yes, definitely." I pull my hair free of the collar. "Mrs. Hattfield only lives fifteen minutes away. I'll be back in time for dinner. Promise."

"It's not getting back I'm concerned about." My mother stares at me, her expression inlaid with concern.

"I know you lost Will, and he was your future. You loved him," Mom says. "But Will was her son. It may not feel like it now, but you'll find someone else. Marry. Have a family. You will move on. She only had one son. The pain of losing a child, you can't imagine it."

I finish tying the belt of my coat with slowed hands and a rapid heartbeat. Will wasn't my future. I wasn't in love with him, and it's a different man I already can't get out of my mind. The one who kissed my tears and rocked my world. I felt lighter after telling Deck the truth, and right now I want to tell someone else.

"Mom, there's something I haven't told you." A self-deprecating laugh escapes me. "Hadn't told anyone really until recently."

I get my nose for news from my mother. A journalism professor at Georgetown, it kind of broke her heart when I chose to attend

Howard. She may have chosen the classroom, and I chose the field, but she still has the inquisitive mind of a journalist, and the questions gather in her eyes and between her brows as a frown.

"Okay." She leans against the stairway bannister in our foyer. "What is it?"

Considering how closely I've guarded this secret, you'd think I'd reveal it with some ceremony. Not on my way out the door with the car already running and warming up.

"Will and I, well . . ." I drop my gaze to the hardwood floor and tug at the fingertips of my leather gloves. "We weren't happy at the end."

I glance up after a few moments of quiet. It's not a stunned silence. It's a knowing one. My mother doesn't look surprised, merely curious, waiting for more.

"I suspected as much," she finally says. "I could tell as soon as I met him that Will was a sad man, but you made him happy. As happy as one person can make another, but ultimately our happiness doesn't hang on other people. We have to first be happy with ourselves, and I don't know that Will ever was."

Now *I'm* stunned. We haven't talked much about Will's suicide. Mom knows I found him in our apartment, but not much else.

"I was getting my things from the apartment because I'd broken off our engagement." The soft admission reverberates through the foyer. "I had agreed to wait to tell everyone. He wanted that, for us to be sure, but I was sure."

Rarely have I seen my mother truly off kilter, but I do now. Her mouth forms a little *O* of astonishment, before she covers it with her hand. She crosses the few feet from the stairs to reach me.

"Oh, baby." She takes my face between her hands. "I had no idea. You've been blaming yourself, haven't you?"

"Mama, he left a note." I lean into the soft comfort of her hand. "For me. It was just to me, and I never told anyone. I kept it. I didn't show the police or . . ."

A sob breaks free from my chest, and tears leak into her palm. "What did I do?" I moan. "Did I . . . should I . . . I don't . . ."

"Shhhh." She pulls me close, the Chanel perfume she's worn for decades a reassurance that breaks whatever tendrils of control I have. My tears pour out, an unrelenting, inconvenient storm. "It's okay, baby. Let it out."

She rocks me in an ancient maternal rhythm that no one teaches; the same one she used when I fell and scraped my knee. When I experienced my first heartbreak. When I buried Will a year ago. After a few moments, she pulls away, hands on my arms so she can look into my face. I sniff and pass my coat sleeve self-consciously under my runny nose.

"No, honey. That's not how it works." She gives a sad shake of her head. "Will was obviously a troubled man, and I know it feels like cause and effect. Like you broke it off and he ended his life. We experience life, all of us, in the bad and the good times and the good people and the ones who hurt us. Everyone does. There are some people life is just harder for than others. Will was one of those, but you told me before how he struggled and didn't always take his medication."

"I don't want to make this about how he failed as a person. I don't want to blame him," I rush to say. "I'm not trying to ease my guilt."

"Well I am." My mother's eyebrows elevate. "Because you have nothing to feel guilty about. Will hurt in a way that we will probably never understand, and for that there is no one to blame. But there's a difference between blame and responsibility. We are each responsible for ourselves. And what Will did, he was responsible for."

That's a distinction I've tried to make to myself more than once, but I always seem to come back to my part in it, and anything I could have done differently. I nod, leaning forward to kiss her cheek before fastening the buttons left undone on my coat.

"I hear you, Mama." I walk to the door and give her one last look over my shoulder. "I'll be back."

"Hey, you aren't planning to tell Mrs. Hattfield that, are you?"

Was I? On some level, I feel like I need to get it off my chest; like I owe her an explanation.

"You told me," my mother says, gripping my hand. "I'm glad you did, because I think you needed that, but that situation is already complicated enough for her. Knowing you and Will broke up only makes it more complicated. May just make it harder, and right now she feels you are the only one in the world close to understanding her pain."

I think of our conversations over the last year. Not many, but each one, a release, a relief for us both.

"Don't take that away from her with information that makes no difference," Mama says. "That does no good. It might make you feel better, but it does nothing for her, and she's your first concern now. That note was to you and you alone. Private. I just want her to be able to move on and accept your comfort. It wasn't your fault. She'll know that, but knowing this would only raise more questions, and she already has enough of those."

I'm playing Mama's words in my head when I pull up to Mrs. Hattfield's. I park my father's Tahoe in the driveway, noting the dying rose bush in front of the house. The grass is longer than the last time I was here, even though it's winter. Her house, always neat and perfectly kept, appears slightly disheveled. I ring the doorbell, waiting. When there is no answer after a few moments, I walk over to the garage, peering in and finding the Cadillac Will used to tease his mother about.

"Are you a pimp, Ma?" he'd ask laughingly. *"Rolling around in your Cadillac."*

I mouth the words, smiling at the image of Will seated in the living room just beyond the doors of this house. One year we helped Mrs. Hattfield trim her tree. Will roasted marshmallows in the fireplace. His mother and I had hot chocolate, and Will had cider. My life with him rushes back to me in vivid detail; the colors, the scents, the touches, the laughs, the tears, the good and the bad. All of it inundates my mind and blurs my vision.

And I miss him.

Not all the hurt we caused each other at the end. I miss the boy I met at a public library, who crushed on me for years without letting me know. Who took me trick or treating with his twelve-year-old cousin for our first date. I laughed with my friends about it, but we all thought it was sweet.

"God, Will." I shake my head, blinking at the tears freezing before they fall. I turn to leave, my steps dragging toward Dad's SUV.

"Avery?"

I turn at the sound of my name, and Mrs. Hattfield stands at the front door, her chin wobbling and her face already streaked with tears. I run, avoiding little patches of ice, needing to get to her. As soon as I'm close, her arms stretch out and she pulls me into her. Her sobs vibrate into my chest.

"I miss him." Mrs. Hattfield weeps unashamedly, her head buried in the collar of my coat. "I miss him so much."

"I know," I whisper, my pain communing with hers. "So do I."

And it doesn't matter if I was wearing his ring. If we were lovers or friends at the end. If he cheated or how we injured each other. All that matters is that I loved him, and so did she. That besides the woman I'm holding, I was closer to him than anyone else on the planet. She and I knew his strengths and his weaknesses like no one else ever did, and can console one another uniquely.

We stand like that for I'm not sure how long. Long enough for the winter cold to bite through my gloves and whip beneath my coat. I pull back and look through the open front door. It's dark in there. No sign of life. No savory smells of food cooking or the pine scent of a live Christmas tree.

"Get your coat, Mrs. H," I command gently. "You're coming home with me."

I didn't get to tell my mom I was bringing someone home for Christmas dinner, but when I arrive, Mrs. Hattfield in tow, she doesn't look surprised and already has an extra plate at the table.

"How'd you know?" I ask her quietly while we set out side dishes.

"I know you." She smiles, pride in her eyes that has nothing to do with anything I've achieved or a goal I've crushed. She's proud of me for who I am, not for what I've done. Mrs. Hattfield and I share a tearful smile at dinner before we say grace. Still sorting through the tangle of guilt and shame and pain and fury, I hope one day soon I'll know me, too.

FOURTEEN

Decker

"I'M STUFFED."

My daughter flops onto the couch beside me in our hotel suite, curly golden hair fanning around her and onto my shoulder.

"Your eyes were bigger than your stomach," I reply, brushing the hair back from her face.

"Grams always says that." Kiera's eyes, the exact color and shape of mine, laugh at me from her mother's face.

"Sure does." I nod and sink deeper into the cushions.

"I wish we'd gone there for Christmas like we were supposed to," she says softly. "To Atlanta to see Grams."

My teeth clamp around the caustic response that springs to my lips. Tara, my ex, used some trumped up excuse about a cheerleading camp Kiera is supposed to attend to make things hard for me. I suspect Kiera doesn't even care about the camp, but she loves her mother.

As she should.

I used to love her mother, too.

I guess.

Sometimes I'm not sure if it was love, lust. Habit? Whatever it was, in the end it wasn't enough.

"Next time." I shoot her a quick smile. "Maybe we'll go see

Grams for Spring break."

She tips her head back and smiles wide, baring her braces, tracks of rubber banded metal glinting in the dimly lit hotel room. I glance at the silver domes covering the remains of our holiday dinner. Not exactly how I wanted to spend Christmas—in a hotel room on the West Coast when everyone who matters to me is on the East. Except my daughter, who matters most of all.

I wonder if it snowed in D.C. Avery's there at her parents' place. I promised myself I wouldn't think about her, but it's easier said than done when you wake up with a throbbing cock, an aching heart and one woman on your mind.

I pull my phone from the pocket of my jeans and open Instagram. She and the other SportsCo anchors are pretty active on social media. It's practically expected, and all of them post for holidays. No new posts from Avery for the last week, though.

"Who's that?" Kiera asks, leaning closer for a better look at the phone. "She's pretty."

I hesitate, never one to lie to my daughter, but unsure how to categorize Avery. If it were up to me, the answer would be easy. Obviously it's not up to me since she and I haven't spoken since that night in the hotel.

"Her name's Avery." I toss the phone on the hotel coffee table. "And we said no phones today, so don't go pulling yours out."

"You started it," she reminds me, eyes bright with curiosity and humor. "Drooling over your *girlfriend*."

"She's not my . . ." I stop myself because dammit if I don't *want* Avery to be my girlfriend. "She's a friend."

Kiera shrugs like it doesn't matter, but she's intuitive, sharp. I've had one-night stands and booty calls since Tara and I divorced, but none of it ever touched my daughter. She's never even seen me date or express interest in anyone, but she's picked up on my interest in Avery. She's growing up. I hate that our choices, mine and Tara's, in many ways made her grow up too fast and deal with things too soon.

Like the fact that love isn't always enough. That sometimes it fades altogether, even for your parents, and it changes your world forever. I know how sad she was when Tara and I divorced; how helpless she felt. She tried to hide it, but it came out in counseling, and we've been open about our feelings with each other ever since.

"Hey. Look at me." I tip up her chin until our eyes meet. "Talk to me. If Avery and I *were* dating, how would you feel about that?"

She blinks a few times and lowers her lashes.

"It's cool." She presses her lips together tight before looking back up at me. "I mean, since you and Mom . . ."

There's a hundred hopes and a dozen questions peppered in the sentence she leaves hanging, and none of my answers would be what she wants to hear.

"You are the most important thing to your mom and me," I assure her. "We'd both do anything for you, but our life together, our marriage, you know that part's over."

"Yeah." The smile she offers seems hard to do. It's not easy. Not natural and mostly for my benefit. "It's cool."

I'm about to dig further when my phone vibrates on the table, drawing my attention and Kiera's. The photo, the contact's name, are clear for us both to see.

Avery.

I grind my teeth together and force my hand to remain still at my side.

Shit.

A week with no word and she calls when I've promised Kiera my complete focus. We agreed to silence our phones before dinner.

"You're not gonna answer?" Kiera asks. "Isn't that your girlfriend?"

"She's not—" I cut myself off when I see the laughter back in her eyes. "We said no phones."

The phone vibrates again, and I can only hope when I call Avery back after Kiera leaves, she'll answer.

"I'll make you a deal," Kiera says. "You get your call. I get my Candy Crush, and then we're back."

I calculate. Under normal circumstances I wouldn't release her from our bargain, but we've both been disciplined and maybe she deserves a little break.

"Deal."

I press the green button to answer my phone, but press it to my chest and give Kiera a wink and smile. "Love you baby girl."

She rolls her eyes and glues her gaze to the phone already in her hands, but grins and mumbles, "Love you, too, Dad."

I step into the bedroom and close the door behind me.

"Avery, hey."

The silence on the other end swells, and I wonder if I caught the call in time or if she hung up.

"Av—"

"I'm here," she cuts in. "I just wasn't sure . . . I'm here."

"Oh. Okay. Uh . . . Merry Christmas."

"Merry Christmas to you, too."

The line goes quiet again. If she's unsure of where this conversation should go, I have suggestions. Number one being that we meet halfway between our coasts and screw all her doubts away. If she agrees to suggestion number one, the rest of the list becomes irrelevant. But I'm not suggesting shit. She wanted space, which I completely understand. As hard as it's been, I've afforded her that time. Ball's in her court. I remain silent, signaling that the next move is hers.

"I, um . . . I saw Will's mother today," she offers stiltedly.

There's a note of sadness, a familiar tremor in her voice. I can only imagine how hard that must have been. She has a lot to work out, but the fact that she's calling me after what had to be a difficult conversation encourages me.

"How was that?" I ask.

"It was . . ." In the pause that follows, I envision her shrugging and biting her bottom lip, dark hair spilling around her shoulders. I wish she was standing in front of me now so I could see if I'm right. "It was tough, but good for us both, I think."

Her chuckle comes across the line and warms me. "She was home alone and that just wasn't right. Will would have wanted . . ."

I'm waiting for her next words, but she lets out a frustrated sigh first.

"I'm sorry. The last thing you want to hear about is Will or his mom or—"

"I want to hear anything you want to tell me, Ave."

She pauses again, her sigh this time one of resignation.

"I didn't tell her about breaking up with Will or how things were between us at the end," she says. "My mother thought that might only make things awkward with the one person Mrs. H feels under-stands what she's going through."

"Your mother sounds like a wise woman," I tell her, keeping my voice even and free of anything that might shut her down. "So you told your mom? How do you feel?"

"Lighter. Between telling you and my mom, I feel lighter." Her laugh is a stunted breath of uncertainty. "Just seeing Mrs. H and cry-ing and us both remembering Will the way we loved him, made me feel better. Does that make sense?"

"Of course, it does. You both probably needed some closure."

"You're right. Closure. I think I got some," she says and then goes quiet for a few seconds. "Oh, Deck, I'm just playing that back in my head and hearing myself. When I said I loved Will, I meant—"

"Whatever you meant is okay." I'm not that much of a selfish, jealous jerk to hold her feelings for Will against her. "Whatever you feel, or felt, is okay."

"Thank you," she whispers, so low I barely catch it. "I've been sorting it all out. I know we had something good once, Will and I, but you were right when you said I couldn't have stayed in that relation-ship. I think I'm finally starting to forgive myself."

She sniffs and clears her throat.

"And to forgive him. I've been so angry with Will, with myself. I'm getting there, but I'm still not . . . I'm not ready, Deck."

"For me, you mean?" I ask, my heart taking a nosedive.

"For us. I'm not ready for anything except tomorrow." Her voice wobbles a little. "And then the next day. And then the next. I need to take it one day at a time for a little longer. I still feel raw in so many places, but I'm getting there. I just think I'd be a hot mess if we . . ."

I gulp down the disappointment and clear my throat.

"Uh, yeah, I get that. Of course," I say, hoping I've disguised the deflation I'm feeling. "Well, I wish you the best and—"

"You *are* the best, Deck," she interrupts softly.

All the words I had queued up to assure her I understand why she needs to walk away from this, from us, wither.

"What does that mean, Avery?"

And why the hell did she call? Just to ruin Christmas? Mission fucking accomplished.

"I'm screwing this up," she says.

"Yeah, a little," I reply, a bit of bite in my words. "If you're just calling to let me down easy, you don't have to. We had a great night, like you said and—"

"I wanted to tell *you*," she interrupts. "Today felt like I had a breakthrough or something . . . shifted. Like I took steps forward when I've felt like I was standing still ever since I found Will. In some ways like I was still in that bathroom with him."

She stops to draw a deep, shaky breath.

"And you were . . . you were the only person I wanted to tell. To call."

Her disjointed explanation sucks all the air out of the frustration swelling inside me, diffusing the irritation and hurt—yes hurt—when I thought she called to stop what had barely started between us, but I desperately wanted to continue.

"I'm glad you had that, Avery," I reply simply. "And I'm glad you called, that you called *me*."

"I think I'll take more steps forward, and that I *will* be ready, but I want . . . I'm just asking for a little more time to clear this fog," she says. "I want to be healthy, whole, when we do this."

When, not if. Good sign.

"Are we ever really whole, Avery?" I ask. "If you figure that shit out, share your secret because most of us live with cracks. I had a career-ending injury, and it healed, but I'll never be the same. I'll never play ball again. Not the way I did before. That spot hurts like a summabitch when it rains. I don't know that I'd call that whole, but I'm walking. I'm not asking you to be whole. I just want to walk with you, baby."

"I think I can do that soon." Her words are so soft, but they fill my ears and land in the vicinity of my heart. "But I'm asking for the time to make sure. My last relationship turned out to be the worst kind of shit show, Deck."

"Ours won't be," I promise without hesitation.

I hear her breath catch, and I want to crawl through the phone, across time zones and kiss her senseless. Fuck her until she forgets everything but us. Fuck the fog away.

"I know it seems like this whole conversation has been about Will and my psychosis," she says, her voice dropping to a husky rasp. "But that's not the only reason I called. I can't stop thinking about you; about that night."

"Dirty thoughts?" I ask hopefully.

"Oh, God," she says with a breathy laugh. "You're ridiculous."

"And you're avoiding the question, Ms. Hughes. Have you or have you not been thinking dirty thoughts about me?"

"Filthy."

"Dammit, Avery," I mutter, running a hand over the back of my neck and glancing at the closed door separating me from Kiera in the other room. "If my daughter wasn't here—"

"Oh, I forgot, Deck. I'm so sorry for interrupting."

"Are you kidding? I'm glad you called. I've been thinking about you all day."

All week. Ever since.

"Dirty thoughts?" she teases.

"Hell, yeah dirty thoughts." I swipe a hand down my face, over my grin. "Filthy as charged."

"Keep it that way," she says, her voice softening even as it heats.

"Oh, what I'm feeling, it'll keep."

FIFTEEN

Decker

"**W**HO'S NEXT?" SEATED ON THE COUCH OF THE SAN DIEGO hotel suite, I stretch my arms above my head.

"It's the last of the day." My assistant Marla looks up from my schedule on her iPad.

"Thank God for that." I crook a grin at her. "Is it too early to start drinking?"

"You drinking?" she scoffs. "What? One of your protein shakes?"

"That *would* be nice." My smile beseeches. "Could you?"

She rolls her eyes, but her smile is good-natured and longsuffering, two things anyone working with me needs to be.

"Let me get you set up for this last interview," she says. "And I'll run up the street to grab one."

"From that place I like, right?" I push my luck.

"Yes, from the place you like." She shakes her head and swipes across the iPad screen. "Gimme a sec and I'll brief you on this last one."

I've lost count of how many reporters I've talked to today for the San Diego Waves' media blitz. I, along with other front office executives, have made ourselves available to the press for questions about the new NBA expansion team, our draft prospects, and the upcoming first season. My canned responses have started losing their shine. The more tired I get, the more I feel like the jock still wet from the shower, no compunction giving half-naked interviews, and less like the guy in the suit scoping talent and making multimillion-dollar decisions. Thank God this is the last of the day.

"It's your old network," Marla says with a smile. "SportsCo."

I stare at her, my heart banging against my rib cage. I'm holding my breath like some lovesick chick waiting to hear Avery's name. She texted me congratulations when my position was announced, but didn't really engage much beyond that, even when I tried. Not that I've tried much in the last three months. She asked for space, and I've given it to her. Though I'm not sure how much longer I can hold out. We only worked in close proximity for three weeks, and we only had one night and a few conversations, but I miss everything about her. I lick my lips before I ask the next question.

"Oh yeah? And uh . . . who'd SportsCo send for the interview?"

"Huh? Oh. Lemme see." Marla trails her finger down the screen until she reaches the bottom. "Mike Dunlov. Ring a bell?"

"Sheesh." I suck my teeth. "Ring a bell? More like a gong. Can't stand that guy."

Disappointment settles on my shoulders, but I square them, refusing to droop. When she's ready she'll come. Avery's too strong-willed for me to force the issue. She knows how good we are together. She's told me more than once she needs time to heal, and I'm giving it to her. That's the thing with a full-court press. You have to know when to apply it, and when to let up, or it's useless.

When there's a faint knock at the suite door, Marla disappears from the sitting room to answer. I look up, grinning at Jerry, the cameraman who danced with Sadie at the Christmas party.

"How you doing?" I stand and wait for him to shift enough of his equipment to shake my hand.

"Good, Deck," Jerry replies with a smile. "Congratulations on all of this."

"Thanks, man. I . . ."

The words disintegrate from my lips and from my mind when Avery, *not* Mike Dunlov, walks into the sitting room with Marla. She looks beautiful as usual, but her hair is different. It's curly, the way I told her I like it. The way it was the day we met in the locker room. She gives me her professional smile, but there's a glint in her eyes that says she knows what I look like under this suit. We are intimately acquainted, and the closer she gets, the thicker the air becomes with our knowledge of each other. Unspoken, the memory of our moans, our rough fucking, our tenderness charges the room, and even though we're having a silent conversation, it becomes obvious that Marla and Jerry sense something.

"Uh . . ." Jerry's eyes move between Avery and me staring at each another. "Where should I set up the camera?"

His question jars Avery, setting her into motion. She assesses the room and directs Jerry. She doesn't look at me again until everything is set up and we're ready to begin. We maintain a friendly formality, just starched enough to be professional, but with the ease of former colleagues. I answer her questions patiently, forcing myself not to stare at her breasts, or the way her waist cinches, or the length of her legs. I don't stare at those things, but I'm *aware* of them. I remember what she looks like and I'm hard as a motherfucker by the end of the interview. To avoid the awkwardness of my hard-on, I stay seated when we're done and Jerry walks over to shake my hand.

"Good to see you again, Deck." He glances at Avery. "You ready?"

She better not go with him. I've been good, controlled myself and given her this interview, even gave her a scoop on things I told no one else. If she tries to leave this room, I'm tying her to the bed.

"Uh, actually . . ." She glances at me, a knowing grin spreading her full lips. "You go on ahead. We're done for the day. I'm gonna catch up with Deck for a little bit."

Or all night long.

Once the door closes behind Jerry, I just stare at her for a few moments, and she stares back at me. It's not awkward. It's anticipation, like we're not sure where to start first, but I just want to begin.

"I like your hair like that," I finally say.

"I know." She tugs at one springy dark curl. "I wore it like this for you."

"For me?" I lean back deeper into the couch, relaxing my legs so she can see the wood I worked so hard to hide from Jerry. Her dark eyes go hot, glancing from my lap to my lips. She takes a step in my direction.

"Stop." I release the word as a command. "There's something you should know before you come any closer."

She links her hands behind her back, pushing her breasts up a little in the silk top she paired with fitted slacks.

"What should I know?" She cocks one brow, waiting.

"Don't come if you're not ready." As much as I want her, as much as I've missed her, I mean every word. "If you're not ready to be with me, to *really* be with me, then don't come because I'm not used to settling, and I'm not starting with you."

She blinks rapidly over the surprise in her eyes, and takes one step in my direction.

"Anything else?" she asks. "Before I come to you?"

"Yeah, I'm not letting you go." I haul a hand through my hair, freshly cut for today's dancing bear media blitz. "Shit, Ave. I've been in relationships before. I've been *married* before, but I've never . . ."

I'm going to sound like a chick. I know it, but I can't stop the words.

"I've never felt like this about anyone else, and I'm not giving you up once I have you. You better get used to that."

Another step, and now she's close enough for me to see tears brightening her dark eyes.

"Is that all?" she asks, her voice rich with emotion.

I nod tersely, not sure she's taking me seriously, but wanting to touch her too much to press the issue. Taking the last few steps and stopping at my knees, she nods to my lap.

"May I?" she asks.

I scoot down another inch, making room for her body to settle over mine. She scoots up until her knees rest on either side of me, and leans forward, pressing her breasts into my chest and her elbows on my shoulders.

"Now let me tell you some things that *you* should know." She brushes a finger over my lips. "You should know that I have missed you every day we've been apart."

I try to ignore what her scent and her warmth and the force of who she is does to me; how holding her is the best thing I've felt since I left New York before Christmas.

"Have you really?" I ask, my tone casual, my heartbeat anything but.

She leans down until her lips hover over mine.

"I did," she breathes over me before going on. "You should also know that I've done a lot of thinking. My relationship with Will taught me a lot. I don't want another relationship . . ."

She doesn't want another relationship? Pain stabs me like a physical cut. Am I willing to be her fuck buddy? The itch she scratches whenever she needs it too badly to ignore?

No, the hell I am not. I make my eyes flinty for our stare off so she won't know she just hurt me more than any woman ever has.

"If this is just some elaborate bicoastal booty call," I say, starting to sit up and pushing her away from me, "Then you can just—"

"Shut up, Deck, and let me finish." She pushes my chest so I fall back onto the sofa. "As I was saying before I was so rudely interrupted."

She pauses to lift one brow. "I don't want another relationship *like I had with Will.*"

Her eyes soften, the brown darkening with emotion.

"I want a relationship where I don't hide and neither do you," she says. "Where we trust each other even with the hard things; the things that break our hearts and cause us pain."

"Avery—"

"Where I never have to worry about you cheating on me and you never have to worry about me cheating on you," she continues. "Where even if we're three thousand miles apart, we're as close as two people can be."

Hope climbs up my chest. I was afraid to let myself hope, but she's here and she's ready, and I can't keep my hands off her even for another second. I grab handfuls of her ass and press her down onto me. We both pant at the first grind of her body into mine.

"That all sounds doable," I rasp.

"'Doable?" she asks breathlessly. "I'm risking a lot here. I'm gonna need something more definitive."

"Really?" My hand moves between us until I can get down her pants, past the barrier of her underwear. She's wet and slick under my stroking fingers. Her hips rock into me, and her head drops back. With my free hand, I loosen the buttons on her blouse. It falls back to reveal a flesh-colored bra of such thin lace I clearly see her nipples.

"I love how big your nipples are." I suck them through the lace, my mouth an eager suction. She moans and slides urgently over me, seeking friction.

"Dammit, Avery, don't make me fuck you like this," I mutter, eyes clenched closed. "I wanted flowers and candles and all kinds of romantic shit when we did this again."

"Fuck flowers." She deals with my belt and slides my pants down, barely waiting for me to lift my hips to help her. "There will be plenty of time for that. Right now, I need you."

She pauses, swallows, her eyes filled with passion, affection and . . . more. I'm afraid to name it, but there is more there.

"I need you," she says again.

"I'm right here, baby." I slide her pants and panties off.

She takes me in hand and pushes down, her walls clinging to me.

"Oh, God." Her head drops back. She rises and falls over me. "Yes."

I slide the cups of her bra over her breasts urging her forward for my bites and licks.

"Shit," I mumble against the silky skin. "Avery, it's been a long time. Slow down or this'll be over before it starts."

She pauses, looking down with a smug grin. "Exactly how long are we talking?"

"If you're asking if I've been with anyone since Christmas, since you." I thrust up, hard and sure. "The answer is no."

I grip her hip, commandeering the pace from beneath her.

"And if you've been letting anybody else in this pussy," I say with grave seriousness. "It's better you don't tell me because that mother-fucker might end up dead."

Her husky laugh breathes over my lips.

"No other motherfucker's been in here."

"Shit." I grimace my frustration. "Why can't I remember a condom with you?"

"It's okay." She leans her forehead into mine. "I'm clean and safe."

I get to fuck Avery raw? I might shed a tear before this is all over.

"Yeah." I nod quickly. "Me, too."

A salacious smile curls her lips. "Then let's go."

She resumes the ride, her face twisting with the effort, with the grind. I flip her onto her back. Eyes locked, we fuck so hard the couch is scooting with the vigor of it. Just inches scraping across the floor, but the sound of it turns me on even more.

She anchors her feet at the small of my back.

"Shit, shit, shit," she chants, eyes rolling back. "Harder, Deck."

"Fuck, baby," I mutter. If I go any harder, I'll break her, but I take her word for it and as soon as I thrust harder, go deeper, her scream pierces the luxurious quiet of the suite. And I'm not far behind, falling over a cliff into the hottest, wildest, longest orgasm of my life.

We lie there on the couch, hot and sweating and panting, laughing between kisses until our stomachs growl. Who would have thought that first night in the locker room all those years ago, that we'd end up like this? We spend the rest of the night feeding each other from room service trays, bathing together, making love, making plans, making promises. Sharing hurts, shedding tears, and loving. Yeah, the words aren't said, but it's there, and we have all the time in the world. For me, there's no doubt it's there. We've both had suffering mixed in with love. We've loved and lost and were never satisfied. But I'm satisfied with her, and I see in her eyes that she's satisfied with me. We both have pasts and we've both had pain, but what we've never had was each other.

But now we do. Thank God, now we do.

EPILOGUE

Avery

I<small>T'S</small> C<small>HRISTMAS</small> D<small>AY</small>, <small>AND IN</small> D.C., <small>MY PARENTS ARE SHOVELING SNOW</small> from the sidewalk. That was me a year ago today. This year, in beautiful stark contrast, I'm watching azure blue waves lick at golden sand. I lean over the balcony to wave at the little girl and older woman down on the shore collecting seashells.

"I'm a lucky bastard," Decker says from behind me, wrapping his arms around my waist and tucking me closer into him. "All my girls under one roof for Christmas."

I turn to face him, reaching up to fiddle with the collar of his shirt.

"Your mother is amazing." I trace the bold planes of his face with one finger. "Now I know where you get those eyes."

"Hmmmm." He bends to kiss the curve of my neck.

"And Kiera is so beautiful." I bend my neck back, giving him better access. "I'm so glad she's spending Christmas with us."

"I'm glad *we're* spending Christmas with us." His big hands slide down my back to squeeze my butt. "This ass. Don't ask how often I think about your ass when we're apart. I might creep you out."

"If I wasn't creeped out by you flashing your junk at me the night we met," I say, laughing against his chest, drawing in the familiar scent of him. "I think you're probably safe."

"Then we won't talk about these either," he says huskily, pushing aside the lapels of my Kimono dress to suckle my breast through my bra.

"Deck." I gasp and clutch his head tighter to me, starting to rock my hips into him in rhythm with his mouth. A seagull's squawk reminds me that, though Deck's beachfront property is private, we're still out in the open. "We have to stop, baby."

"I need you." He growls into the cleave of my breasts before righting the dress. "Stay an extra week."

He knows I can't. The interview I've scored with one of the world's best soccer players is a huge coup. Unfortunately, the interview is in Brazil at the beginning of the year.

"We get seven whole days together," I whisper into the tanned column of his neck. "And we have so much time to make up for."

His sober expression doesn't lighten, and I shake him a little, offering a smile to cajole him into a better mood.

"Deck, come on. You came to D.C. to meet my parents at Thanksgiving. I'm meeting Kiera and your mom for Christmas." I cup his jaw, forcing him to look at me. "We're making this work."

"But when do I get you next?" He laces our fingers together. "The season is about to kick into full gear. It's our first year, so I know we won't make the playoffs, but we're doing better than expected, and I can't let off the gas. My travel schedule—"

"Is part of your job," I cut in. "Just like mine is. We'll see each other every chance we get. That's what we've been doing, right?"

I once dropped everything and raced to LaGuardia where Deck had a layover. We only had an hour, but we made the most of it. I can now say I've been fucked in a men's bathroom. Hard.

No regrets.

"I just want this so bad, Ave." He rubs a thumb over my lip, leaving a trail of tingles. "I want this to work."

"It is working." I tip up on my bare toes to string kisses along his jawline. "We're working, Deck."

"I know, but it could be easier. SportsCo has an LA office," he reminds me, glancing up through those thick lashes. "Couldn't you . . ."

He trails off because we've had this discussion more than once.

"They do have an LA office, but right now they want *Twofer* based in New York." I pause significantly. "I know because I asked."

He pulls back, surprise and pleasure mingling in his eyes. "You asked?"

"I want this to work, too, Deck." I blink at the emotion that overtakes me when I think about how patient he's been the last year. How he helped me so much as I got past Will's death. "I want us to work so much. I love…"

I catch myself. What the actual fuck? We haven't said those words yet. I know them. I believe them. With every fiber of my being, I believe them. I can't imagine spending my life with anyone else, even if right now thousands of miles separate us most of the time. But that's a big step. Those words are a huge step, and the last man I gave them to broke my heart in the worst ways with the worst goodbye I could ever imagine.

Deck doesn't look thrown off by my slip, but just tucks my hair behind my ear and smiles down at me. I know he loves me. His eyes glow with it. I think the only reason he hasn't said it yet is because he wants me to be sure. He knows how fragile I was after Will, and he's handling me like glass.

Not in the bedroom. In bed, he fucks like an animal, and gets no complaints from me.

In every other way, he's been extraordinarily careful with me; extraordinarily patient. And, yes. I love him for it.

I brace my hands on either side of his face, and lock my eyes with his, losing myself in the intoxicating bourbon of his gaze.

"I love you, MacKenzie Decker," I say, my voice, my eyes, my heart steady and unwavering.

He swallows deeply. His hands tighten at my waist, feeling like they'll crush me, but I don't even whimper. I want to feel him any way I can.

"Avery," he finally says. "Baby, I love you so much sometimes I think I'm gonna explode with it."

He dips his head into the curve of my neck, feathering kisses there and into the collar of my dress.

"And I know I'm demanding," he goes on. "Always asking for more of your time, for you to come here more, to meet me on the road. It's not fair—"

"You come to me, too. You travel constantly. I'm always working. We have busy lives, but call me, and there's no place I won't come. This relationship is important to me." I kiss his cheek, scrunch my fingers in the silky gold dappled hair. "You know that."

"I do know," he says, his eyes earnest, sober, loving. "And I don' t take it for granted. I want to make you happy, Ave."

I learned from Will that happiness starts with yourself; that your happiness can't truly hinge on one other person in this world. In the end, other people can't complete us, but can love us in our broken-ness if we let them. There is a happiness you find with another when you're first happy with yourself. The joy of shared struggles and ups and downs and trials and *I'm there for you*, and *you're there for me*. It makes the contentment you find first with yourself even brighter, even deeper. And as we hold each other, the cool beach breeze blow-ing gently over us, I'm reminded of Deck's patience as I figured that out; as I dragged myself out of the mire of guilt and shame and pain.

I have no doubt that's the love Deck and I share.

"I am happy, Deck." I snuggle deeper into my big man, his arms wrapped around me and sheltering me from the whipping breeze. "I'm already happy."

Long Shot Stocking Stuffer

You must read LONG SHOT to appreciate this Christmas-themed bonus material. The events take place after the book.

Get LONG SHOT here: *https://amzn.to/2PrMrqQ*

If you've read it,
did you miss Iris and August's TWO bonus chapters at the end of their book?

You should read that before this bonus material!!!
Go to this link to receive their BONUS Epilogue
www.subscribepage.com/LongShot-bonus

August

THERE'S A MILLION THINGS I LOVE ABOUT PLAYING IN THE NBA. Christmas Day games—not one of them. Christmas Day *away* games, even worse. But that's what we had today. An evening game in New York. So my family wouldn't have to travel on Christmas, Iris, Sarai and I flew in from San Diego yesterday, stayed in a hotel and enjoyed a leisurely Christmas morning. Even though we were away from home, at least we were together. With the game over, and it being so late, we decided to stay in New York tonight.

"Good game, Rook. Nice shot for the win."

Kenan "Gladiator" Ross' compliment comes with his favorite jab. I catch his over-the-shoulder smirk in the Knicks' guest locker room.

"I got too many seasons under my belt," I tell him, buttoning my shirt. "For you to still be calling me Rook."

"Nah." Fresh from the shower, he towels residual water from his head and neck. "Breath still smelling like Similac."

The few guys left in the locker room snicker, and I shake my head, chuckling and packing my bag.

"At least I'm not *a veteran* scared to talk to a girl I'm crushing on," I say.

"Ohhhhh," Denny, the center we picked up over the summer says, putting a fist to his mouth and laughing. "You got a *crush*, Glad? Who?"

Kenan narrows his eyes at me, but a good-natured grin lifts one corner of his mouth.

"He's lying," Kenan says, pulling a sweater over his head. "I'm a grown ass man. I don't have crushes."

"Oh, then you don't care that your *not-crush* is coming to Deck's Christmas party tonight?" I ask.

Since the game finished so late, MacKenzie Decker, our president of basketball operations, invited those of us staying in New York to a party at a hotel nearby.

I pull my phone from my pocket. "I'll just call Iris and tell her not to bring—"

Kenan snatches my phone and laughs. "Fuck you, August."

"That's what you get for calling me Rook." I grab my phone, grin and turn to close my locker.

Kenan steps closer and leans one huge shoulder against the neighboring locker.

"So is she coming to the party for real?" he asks, voice lowered. "Or you just being a dick?"

"Sorry." I turn fake-innocent eyes his way. "Who we talking about?"

Not the most affable man under the best of circumstances, Kenan looks like I'm thinning his patience. His whole face seems to tighten, which perversely makes me want to jerk his chain even more.

"Alright, alright." I hold up my hands as if warding off a blow. "Don't hit your boy. Yeah, Lotus is coming. Least, last I heard from Iris, she was."

"Cool." Kenan nods, and his typically impassive expression gives way to what looks like anticipation.

"If you like her, why not just talk to her, man?" I ask, adjusting my gym bag on my shoulder.

"She's very good at letting me know she wouldn't be into it, into me," Kenan says wryly. "Without even saying a word."

He shakes his head and offers a bemused shrug. "There's just something about her. I don't know. The last thing I should be thinking about is some chick, considering the shit the last one is putting me through."

"Bridget still tripping?"

"Tripping?" Kenan scoffs. "Man, not only is she holding up our divorce, but she's moving my daughter here to New York."

"Damn. You talked to Deck? You know his ex pulled a stunt like that. Moved his daughter from the East coast to LA." A dry laugh rattles my chest as we make our way out of the locker room and down the tunnel leading to the private parking lot. "Lucky for us. He probably wouldn't have come to the West Coast if she hadn't."

"I haven't talked to much of anyone except my lawyers." Kenan grimaces. "My drama's been talked about, dragged through the press enough already."

I wince because TMZ couldn't get enough of Bridget's affair with Kenan's former teammate. For someone as private and reserved as Kenan, the inescapable salacious coverage was his worst nightmare.

"Hey, I know that was a shit show," I say. "But it's died down. Old news."

"You think it'll stay dead once she re-airs our dirty laundry on reality TV?" Kenan asks, a bitter edge to his voice.

I stop in my tracks and face him, searching his stony expression in the poorly lit tunnel.

"What the hell?" I wait for him to stop and face me. "What do you mean?"

"The reason she's moving to New York is to be on one of those reality shows about ballers' wives or some shit." He sucks his teeth, annoyance in every tense line of his six-foot-seven frame. "We're this close to a divorce and haven't lived together in over a year, and she signs on as a baller's wife? What baller?"

"Glad, man, I'm sorry."

We resume walking to the lot and Kenan shrugs.

"I'll deal with it," he says. "The worst part is how it affects my daughter. She's old enough to hear all the shit about us, but not old enough to really understand. She still doesn't get that Bridge and I will never be together again."

"I don't get her," I say. "Bridget, I mean. She had everything. Great husband. Great kid. Great life, and she threw it all away for what?"

"For *who* is a better question. Dude's not even checking for Bridget now, and from what I hear, he just got engaged. I mean, I'm no picnic. I'm not an easy guy to get close to. I know that. And we had our issues, but I never thought . . ."

Kenan frowns and squeezes the bridge of his nose.

"Anyway, count your blessings, Rook. You got a good woman."

Just the thought of Iris waiting for me at the end of this tunnel fires my blood and squeezes my heart in my chest. Count my blessings? Every day. And pretty soon, we'll have another blessing, though Iris and I have kept that to ourselves for now.

"Yeah, she and Sarai are the best things that ever happened to me," I reply, shooting Kenan a grin. "They're here. We won't stay long at the party. We have Sarai with us."

"Surprised you're not heading down to Baltimore to see your folks?"

"My mom and stepdad are in Hawaii, if you can believe it. Jared gave them a trip for their anniversary, and they decided to go there for Christmas. Hey, they're both off for the holidays, so I guess it works for them. At least we were all together for Thanksgiving."

"And Jared? What are he and Banner up to for Christmas?"

"Staying west. They're spending Christmas with her folks in San Diego," I say. "So with my family scattered all over the place this year, New York's as good a place as any to land. Especially with that W we got tonight."

We fist bump, celebrating another win. This season is already going better than last. We just knew we'd make the playoffs last year, but ultimately fell short. We've been building this franchise ever since I came to the NBA, and I think, I *hope*, this time we'll make the playoffs.

"Hey, start counting," Kenan says, nodding to the black SUV where Iris and Sarai wait for me. "There's your blessings."

I hope I never get used to the passion and protectiveness that surges through me when I first see Iris. Though I'm guilty of what my old coach termed the impulsivity of youth and the quick temper that often comes with it, I've never considered myself a violent person. But had I known how Caleb was hurting Iris when she was with him, I think I might have killed him. That sounds harsh and wrong, but seeing that season of our lives through hindsight—the sadness lurking behind Iris' eyes, the way she'd startle when I touched her unexpectedly, the scars she explained away—futile rage consumes me for a second. Futile because there's no outlet for it. Caleb is dead, and I've never felt sorry about that.

As soon as we join my girl at the SUV, I pull Iris close and kiss her hair. She snuggles into me briefly, then tips up to kiss the corner of my mouth. Her eyes are hot and hungry when they meet mine. We made love this morning before Sarai woke up and bounded into our bed at the hotel, but it's like we've gone weeks, not hours, without making love.

"Good game," she whispers to me, discreetly brushing a hand over my chest under my coat.

My muscles tighten under the light touch of her fingers. I'm tempted to skip this party. I want her to myself in every position doing every dirty thing we can dream up. But she's already changed and she looks so beautiful. Her dark hair has grown, and it spills nearly to her waist, thick and shiny. The gold dress of sequins molds her slim frame and caresses every curve. Gold stilettos give her a few inches and further define the sexy muscles of her calves.

"Damn, you look good," I whisper into her ear.

"So do you," she whispers back, her hand drifting down between us under my coat to squeeze my dick. "Good enough to eat."

Holy shit.

"You two just gonna hump each other in the parking lot?" Kenan asks, threading laughter through the words. "I'm here for it, but you might want to remember the youth among us."

Iris and I both turn our heads to find Sarai staring at us over the half-up window of the SUV. The other most important girl in my life.

"Hey, Princess," I say, returning her wide, missing-a-tooth grin. "How'd I do tonight?"

"You did good, Daddy." She wags one tiny finger. "Mommy says you still need to work on that D."

Kenan's laughter booms in the nearly-empty parking garage.

"From the mouths of babes," he says. "I keep trying to tell him that jump shot will only go so far. He better bow up."

"You're right." I walk Iris over to the car. "I should listen to my elders."

"Boy, I'll be playing til I'm forty if I want," Kenan says, patting his famous rock-hard slab of abs under his sweater. "The older you get, the smarter you better play."

"Okay, okay," Iris says, laughing and turning toward the open door. "How about you guys talk ball when we get to the party?"

I help her step onto the running board and into the back seat. I buckle her in and rest a hand on her stomach.

"How are we doing today?" I ask, an irrepressible grin taking over my whole face. I've been smiling for a week straight. I've probably been smiling in my sleep, I'm so thrilled.

"Um . . . *we're* fine," Iris whispers, casting a cautious glance over my shoulder at Kenan. "And aren't *we* supposed to be waiting to share *things?*"

"Yeah. Right." I turn to face Kenan and decide to rib him a little before we part ways for the party. "Iris, is Lotus still coming? Kenan wanted to know."

Kenan's smile drops, and it looks like he wants to turn all that power and muscle to grinding me to dust.

"What?" I offer him a nonchalant shrug and wide eyes. "You *did* ask."

A muscle ticks under the taut skin of his jaw.

"She's coming, yeah," Iris says, leaning forward a little to smile at Kenan. "She's swinging through just for a little while."

"I'll see you guys there," Kenan says without acknowledging Iris's statement. He gives her a tight smile, glares at me, and turns to walk toward the SUV the team sent to take him to the party.

"You're awful, teasing him like that." Iris belies her scolding with a mischievous smile. "But I did kinda love the look on his face."

"Right? What did Lotus say when you told her Kenan was coming to the party?"

"Weeeelll," Iris says, drawing the word out, a sneaky grin lighting her pretty face. "I didn't exactly mention it."

"Oh, this should be interesting."

The car pulls off and heads for the parking lot exit. I turn my attention to Sarai, who has been uncharacteristically quiet.

"You okay over there, Princess?" I push her hair back and lift her little chin to study her unique violet-blue eyes. She nods wordlessly, and long lashes droop lazily over drowsy eyes.

"She's tired," Iris says. "But refused to skip the party altogether. Always afraid she's going to miss something. I don't want to stay long, though."

Iris rolls a lust-filled glance from my head to my toes, and my dick gives a knowing twitch.

She bites her bottom lip and looks at me from under her lashes. "I want to get back to the room. We have unfinished business, Mr. West."

I glance from Sarai, watching us with sleepy interest to the rearview mirror, checking if the driver is tuned into our conversation. I lean over, nudging Iris' hair back with my nose and biting her ear lobe. A shiver runs through her.

"You are so damn horny lately," I whisper. "Is it the baby?"

Saying it out loud, even just for the two of us, feels amazing. We're having a baby. We haven't told Sarai she's getting a little brother or sister. We haven't told my parents or Jared and Banner. We've held it close like a secret for the last few days. A secret we made, just the two of us, and for a few days at least, it belongs only to us.

"The hormones may heighten things," she whispers back, her eyes, glinting with amber and onyx. "But I've always wanted you."

"And there hasn't been a moment since the night we met that I haven't wanted you."

God, it's true. Ships that pass in the night. Star-crossed lovers. Whatever you call us, however you'd characterize our relationship before, we're together now. And the ache I lived with for years, the longing to be with her is a distant memory. I have the career I've wanted since I was old enough to hold a basketball, married to the woman of my dreams, a daughter who is mine in every way that counts, and now another on the way.

Count my blessings. I run out of fingers, out of hands, out of ways to count all the good in my life.

"We're here," Iris says, her sweet, deep voice jolting me out of my thoughts.

She squeezes my thigh and trails kisses under my jaw. "And remember we're not staying long."

Our gazes hold, our eyes making promises for later tonight. I scoop up Sarai and she yawns so wide and long her eyes water.

"We don't have to go to the party," I tell her, smoothing her hair back. "If you're too tired."

"No, I want to go," she says, forcefully perking up.

"Okay, but we can't stay long." I fake a yawn to match hers. "Daddy needs to rest. I'm so tired."

"You are?" Surprise widens her sleepy eyes.

"I am, and we gotta be up early tomorrow for our flight back to California."

"Good. It's cold here," she mumbles into the wool of my coat. "I want my swimming pool."

"I know, baby." I shift her on my hip and take Iris' hand when we enter the hotel.

"That looks like our tree." Sarai points to the center of the lobby.

"It's beautiful," Iris says, looking around the lobby, outfitted for Christmas with lights and a brightly decorated tree. Ahead of us, a hotel attendant waits at a stand with a list. He checks our names off, walks us to the private elevator and punches in a code.

"Oh!" Iris says, holding the elevator door. "Can you make sure Lotus DuPree and guest are on your list?"

The attendance consults his list, confirming with a nod and a smile.

"Aunt Lo's coming?" Sarai asks, perking up. Those two have a special connection. Iris is just praying Lotus doesn't teach our daughter any of her voodoo tricks when we're not looking.

"Yes." Iris fixes her eyes on the illuminated ascending numbers. "For a little bit."

It seems half the San Diego Waves team is here, along with several guys from the front office. I spot Deck with his arm around Avery Hughes. He and the SportsCo anchor no longer hide their relationship, and I'd lay bets we'll be hearing wedding bells for those two soon.

Every corner of the penthouse suite is decorated and occupied. I count three Christmas trees, two bars, and I've stopped counting people.

"Full house," Iris says, taking Sarai's hand when I set her on her feet. "Oh, good. There's a few other wives and kids here."

"Will you have to play on Christmas next year, Daddy?" Sarai asks.

"Let's hope so." I offer a wry grin. "It usually means people want to see your team play, and I hope people keep wanting to see the Waves."

"We'll just cross our fingers that next year will be in San Diego," Iris says, smiling and stroking Sarai's hair. "You sleepy, Princess?"

"Not anymore," Sarai replies, her eyes roving the sparkling room stuffed with well-dressed adults laughing, talking, even a few gathered around a baby grand at the other end of the suite and singing Christmas songs. We listen to a few carols, make the rounds and talk to mostly people from the team, grazing food and sipping drinks.

"Remember we're only staying for a little bit," I tell Sarai, but look meaningfully at Iris. I don't want all this Christmas cheer to derail the hot fuck we've penciled in.

Iris tosses me an amused glance, and twists her lips into a knowing wry curve.

"Bo!"

Iris' head turns sharply at the nickname only Lotus uses. Her face lights up as soon as she spots her cousin, who's more like a sister.

"Lo!" she calls back. The cousins close the space separating them with a few quick strides, arms outstretched.

"Heyyyyy, girl." Lotus returns Iris' squeeze, closing her eyes and burying her face in my wife's hair for a second. Their embrace goes beyond the typical greeting. Even so physically different, there is something about them that is the same. Iris, with her lighter skin and long, silky hair, still seems somehow genetically connected to Lotus with her golden brown skin and trademark platinum braids gathered into a low side knot at her neck. Connected by more than genetics, but by something deeper. Both swipe at tears and sniff even as they smile into each other's eyes. Lotus pulls back, inspecting Iris' face with such intent you'd think she's reading a diary entry.

"Something's different," she says after a few seconds. "What's going on with you?"

I don't understand Lotus' intuition; her way of seeing beneath the surface of things, but it's consistent. Like Lotus, I refuse to believe in her voodoo nonsense, but there's no denying she has some inexplicable sixth sense. Tonight, though she hasn't figured it out yet, it's probably that Iris is pregnant.

"Girl, what?" Iris says lightly, waving her hand dismissively, playing it off. "Maybe I cut my hair since you saw me last. That's probably it."

"No, it's something else." Lotus narrows her eyes and runs a glance from Iris' head to her toes. "I'll figure it out."

"Whatever, Lo." Iris rolls her eyes and grins. "You haven't even said hello to your biggest fan yet."

Lotus immediately turns her full attention to my daughter, and they both squeal like little girls. Well, Sarai *is* a little girl. Lotus is just genuinely thrilled to see her.

"Have you been a good girl?" Lotus asks. It's not the teasing adults usually use to ask children that question. There's a weight to it, like Sarai's answer matters. And Sarai answers in kind, her little face mirroring the seriousness of Lotus' expression when she nods that she has been.

"Good!" Lotus brightens like someone turned on the Christmas lights. "Because I have your gift."

"Yay!" Sarai claps and jumps up and down in her Christmas sweater and skirt. Her little hand pops out, ready for whatever goodies Lotus has for her.

"Oh, darn it.," Lotus says, a frown pinching her thick brows together. "Where's my bag?"

"Right here, Lo," a man says from behind me. If Upper Eastside private school had a sound, it would be this man's voice. I turn to find a guy, a little over average height, with his blond-streaked chestnut hair gathered into a man bun. A grin creases his pretty boy face and he hands Lo a coat and small clutch bag.

"You took off running and literally left me holding the bag," the guy continues.

"Oh, sorry." Lo takes the items with a quick smile. "Guys, this is Chase Montclair. He's one of New York's most promising photographers."

She shoots him a wry, teasing smile. "At least that's what he keeps telling everybody."

"Very funny." Chase extends his hand in greeting, and Iris and I both shake it. "Hey. Merry Christmas."

He has soft hands, like the hardest thing he's ever done is lift that camera. I shouldn't judge, but I'm probably biased because of the way he keeps looking at Lotus like she's Christmas dinner. Kenan has no claim to Lo, and they've only met a handful of times, exchanged so few words, but I still wish Chase wasn't here with Kenan on the way.

"Grabbed you a drink, babe," Chase says, proffering a glass to Lotus.

Babe? Iris and I exchange a look, both of us lifting eyebrows high.

"Ooooh. Aperol," Lotus sighs and takes a long sip. "You know me so well."

Does he? Who is this guy?

By the curious glances Iris darts between Lotus and Chase, she's as clueless as I am. I catch a glimpse of Kenan entering, taller than just about everyone, which is saying something in a roomful of basketball players. His customary scowl clears when he sees me. Lo is as petite as Kenan is tall, so I don't think he sees her through all the trees present until he's right up on us.

"Rook, long time, no see," he jokes and daps me up. His eyes drift around our small circle until they land on Lotus. Seems every time they're in a room together, which hasn't been often, a staring match ensues. Tonight is no different. A wordless war is being waged between them. Kenan watches Lotus like she might take off running at any minute, which usually happens. She stares back like a wily fox who finds herself in a trap, but isn't out of options yet.

"Dude, you've got great forearms," Chase says, snapping the living thread stretching between their stares. Kenan shifts his glance from Lotus to the soft, pale hand caressing Lotus' neck, and then to Chase's face.

"Excuse me?" One arrogant lift of Kenan's brow sends some grown men scurrying, but Chase is too oblivious to know he should be cautious with his next words.

"Your forearms," Chase repeats, gesturing to where Kenan has pushed up the sleeves of his sweater, baring the whipcord muscle and veins of his lower arms. "Sorry. I'm a photographer. Noticing shit like that is my job."

His comment falls into silence about as friendly as a vat of acid. Kenan tilts his head, studying Chase like he's some other species. Maybe Millennial Manbunian. I'm privately congratulating myself on that bit of clever dopeness, when Lotus makes her move. Her move being to peace out.

"Speaking of your job," she says, finishing her Aperol and placing the glass on a passing tray. "We should get going. My boss is throwing a Christmas party tonight and we're supposed to be there. He's really big on these parties."

"But we just got—"

"Stay if you want," Lotus interrupts Chase's protest. "I'm out."

Lotus is one of the fiercest women I know, and I've never seen her run from anything. I have no idea why, but she's running from Kenan. Iris offers him a subtle shrug, silently apologizing for something that isn't her fault. Kenan doesn't acknowledge her, but grabs a whiskey from a server walking past. He holds the liquor in one hand, crosses his arms over his chest and turns his glance back to Lotus and Chase.

I survey the festive opulence of the penthouse suite, taking in the guys I battle with on the court night in and night out. We'll have the briefest of reprieves for the holiday. In just two days, we're back on the road for the last two thirds of a grueling eighty-two game season. I want to go back to our hotel, put Sarai to bed, fuck my wife like it's nineteen-ninety-nine, even though we're well past that, and tomorrow, go home. There's a cluster of suited men supplicating around Decker. I see that dude all the time, and will see him next week back in Cali. There's no reason to stay.

"I'm with Lo," I bend to whisper in Iris's ear. "Let's be out."

Iris

"Let's be out," August whispers to me.

I am so down for that. Sarai's initial fascination with the holiday scene and all her daddy's "giant" friends has faded into exhaustion. She'll sleep through the night, and if we're lucky, she'll sleep in. And if I'm lucky . . .

It feels like hot steam being carried through my blood, the way I want August tonight. These hormones . . . I can't get enough of my husband.

He has not complained.

I'm pregnant. A bubble of joy expands around my heart. I look at August, the man literally of my dreams through the darkest season of my life, and my daughter, the only good that came from my relationship with Caleb. I have been content for a long time, but now, this new life growing inside of me, is my cup running over. Such great joy spilling over the sides and saturating my life with more blessings.

I blink away tears. Lotus' sharp eyes have already seen more than I was ready to reveal. And then it hits me, I want her to know. August and I agreed that we would carry our secret to New Year's Eve, and then tell only those closest to us, but it's so rare I see Lotus these days. My life is filled with a demanding career I've carved out for myself, raising my daughter, and sharing every drop of happiness with my husband on the West Coast. And Lotus lives at warp speed here in New York, traveling to Paris, Milan, Hong Kong. She's become that designer's right hand of sorts. Who knows when we'll see each other again.

I tip up on my toes and slip my fingers into the abundance of August's dark, silky curls, longer than his mama prefers, and exactly how I like it.

"Hey," I whisper to him. "I know we said we'd wait til New Year's to tell everyone, but what do you think about me telling Lotus tonight?"

He turns his head, and only a breath charged with what I've had to deny myself all day separates us. He dips and kisses me. The kiss, light though it is, feels like gasoline poured on the fire in my belly. I pull back, panting, breasts heaving. His smile is knowing and his eyes ravenous. He'd give me the moon if I asked for it right now.

"Whatever you want," he replies, sliding his wide palm down my back to rest at the curve of my ass. "Just promise we'll leave in the next two minutes. I need to be inside you."

I close my eyes against a wave of want and nod jerkily. He's barely touching me, but electricity fans out from his fingers at my waist and draws my nipples tight. My pussy clenches and contracts with the desire he stirs in me effortlessly.

"We're leaving, too," I tell Lotus. I clear my throat of the huskiness and continue. "It's been a long day. I'm sorry we didn't have more time together this trip."

"Yeah, but I'm in LA next month." Lotus smiles down at Sarai, tucking a lock of thick hair behind her ear. "Now are you sure you were a good girl because I can't give you the Christmas present if you weren't."

"I was good." Sarai strains on her toes, eyes stretched wide and earnest. "Mommy, tell her I've been good."

Everyone in our little circle laughs. The grim line of Kenan's mouth even yields a small smile. I don't know what it is between him and Lotus, but she is avoiding it like the plague.

"Okay," Lotus says. "Well if you've been good."

She goes down on her knees, careless of the obviously expensive leather dress molding her petite curves. I understand why Kenan keeps staring at her. I've seen her all my life, but she seems to be blossoming even more before my eyes. Her face is expertly made up, a cat eye emphasizing the natural slant of eyes fringed with fake lashes and lined with mystery. Her skin, honey and cinnamon, glows against the platinum braids gathered in an elegant knot at her neck.

She reaches into her clutch and draws out a pale pink sachet bag with a cream silk drawstring tie.

"What is it?" Sarai asks, her eyes bright as gold coins.

"That's why you open it, silly," Lotus laughs and puts the bag in Sarai's tiny palm.

For some reason, I find myself holding my breath. The satchel stirs a memory I'd forgotten. Of Mimi giving us *gris gris* rings in bags that looked like this. My glance zips to Lotus, only to find her looking up at me, searching my face for approval. I caress the silver ring on my right hand and remember the painful days without it; when Caleb stole and hid it from me. And I remember the sense of rightness when it rested on my finger again. I give Lotus a small nod and blink back tears again.

Damn hormones. Horny *and* emotional.

"A ring!" Sarai's mouth makes a delighted "o," and her smile stretches across her little face. "For me?"

"Just for you," Lotus says, still on her knees. "I made this ring for you."

"You made it?" I ask, my pulse skidding. Mimi made ours, and I didn't even know Lotus knew how.

"Yes, I made it," Lotus returns solemnly, her eyes fixed on Sarai's face. "Look at me, little girl."

Sarai looks up, and the wonder of the gift dims when she meets the seriousness of Lotus' expression.

"You remember Mimi?" she asks, and I recognize the shadow that passes through Lotus' eyes as sorrow. She still grieves our great-grandmother who raised her. Even though she was so young when we took shelter in the bayou with Mimi, Sarai remembers her. She made quite an impression on everyone who crossed her path.

Sarai nods, her gaze locked with Lotus'.

"She made my ring." Lotus raises the ring finger of her left hand where she wears her *gris gris*. "And she made your mama's, too."

Sarai looks up and over her shoulder at me, her eyes dropping to the ring even now I'm stroking.

"It's protection and you never take it off," Lotus says, her tone firm, serious. *"Tu comprends, oui?"*

Hearing the French tongue Mimi taught her when she was so young seems to startle Sarai. I'm much less fluent than Lotus. I don't use French at all really, but Sarai first learned to talk in the bayou with Mimi, and half her first words were English and the other half, French. Looking at her, between my German father and her blond, blue-eyed father, our Creole heritage has been so diluted, you'd never know Sarai's Creole ancestors hail from the belly of the Bayou.

"Oui," she replies softly.

"Is that some voodoo shit, Lo?" Chase asks, the cocksure grin on his handsome face at odds with the hesitation in his voice.

I'd forgotten he was even there. The world had narrowed down to my daughter and my closest relation, and the significance of the gift she was bestowing. I'd forgotten about Kenan, too, whose attention remains fixed on Lotus.

Lotus stands, smoothing the creases in the leather dress from squatting on the floor.

"Shut up, Chase," she says easily, the look she offers him indulgent. "Don't talk about things you don't understand."

"Voodoo?" Kenan asks, a deep vee between his eyebrows. "Like potions and spells voodoo?"

Lotus looks way up at him, meeting his skepticism directly.

"What do you know about it?" she asks, one sleek brow cocked in challenge. "Spells and potions and hexes and Hollywood?"

"I know it's not real," Kenan scoffs.

She steps closer until she stands right in front of him, tipping her head back to meet his eyes. Even in heels she barely reaches his shoulder.

"Not real?" Lotus smiles like a cat toying with a ball of yarn. "How do you know I haven't cast a spell on *you*?"

Something flares, sparks in the dark depths of Kenan's eyes and he bends until their faces almost align.

"Because a woman like you," he says softly, so softly that I think only Lotus and I can hear. "Doesn't need spells to make a man want her."

In my head, I scratch a point for Kenan on my air scoreboard. *Good one.*

The seconds draw out like an accordion as they stare at one another, and I wouldn't be surprised if the lights flicker there is so much power in the silent exchange. Lotus rubs her *gris gris* ring with the pad of her thumb and finally snaps the thread between them.

"Let's go, Chase," she says abruptly, deliberately shifting her eyes from Kenan to her friend, or whatever he is.

"We're leaving, too," August says. "We can walk down together."

Kenan drags his glance from Lotus and does the man hug thing with my husband.

"I'll see you back in SD," August tells him.

"Yeah, see you Monday in the gym," Kenan says absently, his eyes tracking Lotus and Chase, who are munching a handful of hors d'oeuvres at the door on their way out.

"Oh, and Kenan?" August says.

"Yeah, what's up?"

"For the record," August says, his grin cocky. "You definitely have a crush."

Kenan's eyes slit, but he yields a grin. He reaches down to cover

Sarai's ears and says softly, "Fuck you, Rook."

I give Kenan a quick hug goodbye, and we walk off to catch Lotus and Chase and all walk to the elevator together.

"So you're on your way to your boss' party?" I ask Lotus while the elevator descends.

"Yeah." She laughs and rolls her eyes. "He loves parties and usually recruits me to help, but I told him I had family in town and would roll through later."

I nod, relishing the news I have to share. Now that we've decided I can tell her, I'm like a kid with a secret, about to burst with it.

When we reach the lobby, we wait for the driver to come with our car. I grab Lotus by the elbow and pull her to the side while she and Chase wait for their Uber.

"Hey, I want to tell you something."

"Sure." Lotus smirks. "Is this about your new 'haircut'?"

I just stare at her for long seconds, wondering if . . . no. She can't know.

"Girl, do you already know—"

"No, it's not like that." She looks uncomfortable for a minute. "It doesn't work like that."

"It?" I probe, watching her closely. "Are you . . . *practicing*, Lo?"

She knows what I mean. I'm asking if she's actually practicing like Mimi did, like so many of the women in our family practiced voodoo until our mothers abandoned it. I don't even believe in it, but Lotus and I see many things differently.

"No." She barks out a laugh. "Girl, when would I find time for it with *my* life? It's not something you dabble in. It's something you devote yourself to. I just . . . get a strong sense sometimes."

She gives me a pointed look.

"Like with your haircut," she says lightly. "Now spill it."

I don't even know what to make of all that, so I just shake my head dazedly and lean forward to tell her my secret.

"I'm pregnant."

Lotus pulls back to stare at me, her mouth gaping open. I feel the tiniest thrill that she really didn't know for sure, and relish her delighted squeal.

"Bo, oh my God!" She draws me into a scented hug. "I'm so happy for you. Oh, gosh. I'm gonna be an auntie . . . again!"

"I know! Crazy, right?"

"Does Sarai know yet?" she asks softly, glancing at my daughter already asleep on her father's shoulder.

"No, we're telling everyone on New Year's Eve." Tears blur my vision for a second. "But seeing you after so long . . . I needed to tell you in person. You're the only one who knows."

Answering tears shimmer over her dark eyes, and she presses her lips tightly together.

"Thank you, Bo," she whispers. "That means a lot."

"Iris," August calls, dipping his head toward the waiting SUV. "Car's here, babe."

Lotus gives him a double thumbs up, and a smile tugs at his full lips.

God, those lips. I want them all over me.

"We gotta go," I say abruptly.

"Okay, and I meant it about catching up when I come with JP, my boss, out to LA next month."

I start walking backward toward the car, keeping my eyes on Lo and slanting her a teasing grin.

"You gonna try to see Kenan while you're out there, too?"

Lotus's smile fades, the light in her eyes flickers and she gestures for Chase when their Uber pulls up.

"Not a chance in Hell," she answers.

"I don't get you." I stop my back stepping to hold her stare. "He's a great guy. And he's handsome. You don't think he's handsome?"

Lotus lets Chase climb into the back seat of the Uber ahead of her and pauses, facing away and turning her head, showing me her profile, not her expression.

"I think he's magnificent," she says softly.

Before I can say as much as a "what the heck," she ducks into the car and it pulls away.

We're quiet on the short drive from Deck's party to our hotel, which is only a few blocks away. We're both loathe to accidentally wake Sarai. If she wakes up, it will take forever to answer all her questions and get her back asleep. We need her to stay down so we can handle this ache that has been throbbing between us all night. An ache we cultivated with every stolen touch and lingering glance.

I *very carefully* tug Sarai's clothes off and slip her nightgown over her head, watching her face for signs of stirring. She's out cold.

Yes! Mama's getting some!

I reach to turn on the bedside lamp so she won't be frightened if she wakes up in the middle of the night, and the light glints over her new *gris gris* ring. There's this constant tug of war between what I believe to be true with my rational mind, and the undeniable realities of my heritage. Maybe it was my imagination that I was actually safe when I wore the ring Mimi gave me. And the leashed power I sense in Lotus sometimes, the gleam of ancient wisdom in her eyes—maybe that's all in my mind, too.

Even though Lotus seems to be the reckless free spirit, taking all the risks I shy away from, she has a compass that never ultimately seems to steer her wrong. I adamantly objected when she dropped out of Spelman to pursue the opportunity in New York, but she knew it was right for her, and even enrolled in FIT once in New York for her Associate's degree in design. If she were a cat, she'd have nine lives and always land on her feet.

I lift Sarai's tiny limp hand and kiss the ring before leaving the room and quietly pulling the door closed.

When I enter the hotel master suite, August's broad, naked shoulders are pressed into the headboard, and his caramel-kissed curls flop into slate gray eyes. The million-thread count hotel sheets puddle at his lean hips and caress the stack of muscles over his abs.

"Let me save you the guesswork," he says, his smirk inviting me to leave any inhibitions at the door. "I am naked under here."

I chuckle and walk to the edge of the bed, bending so one knee dips into the mattress.

"And let me save you the guesswork," I say, tugging the sequin dress over my head. "I'm naked under here."

I ignore the groan that escapes his lips at the sight of me in my thong and tiny bra.

"Well, almost naked." My eyes never leave his while I unfasten the front snap of my strapless bra and slide the scanty underwear over my hips and down my legs.

"Am I coming to get you?" August asks, his breaths growing labored, sexual tension snapping in the small space separating us. Just the length of the bed, but it feels like he's a hundred miles away.

"How about I come get you?" Naked with my hair hanging over my shoulders, brushing my already tight nipples, I can barely make myself go slow. I want to fling myself at him. To jerk the sheet away and impale myself on him. Ride him until we both come so hard we see stars. Instead I draw out every move, stretching my advance like notes held, sustained. His eyes heat, setting my skin on fire everywhere they touch me. I feel his glance like a physical thing, stroking me into a frenzy I can barely contain. By the time I reach him, I'm so wet, the insides of my thighs are damp. Holding my stare, August slips his hand between my legs and massages the wetness into my swollen lips.

"Well looka here. A gift for me?" he asks, his laugh low and rough. "You shouldn't have."

God, he's so beautiful, inside and out, and I can't believe he's mine sometimes. I still wake up some mornings expecting to be trapped in the nightmare that was once my life, and tears of gratitude, of awe fill my eyes, sometimes spill over when I realize that I'm literally living the dream. Maybe that will always happen from time to time. You don't escape the hell I was confined to unscarred, unburnt. You live with those memories, learn from those mistakes and make the best life you can.

And this life with August, exceeds my every hope.

"We're gonna have a baby," I whisper, rolling my hips over his exploring fingers.

"I know." He sits up and gently presses my shoulders until my back is against the mattress and he hovers over me. "Cause for celebration, I'd say."

His lips closing over one nipple while he rolls the other between his fingers draws a whimper from me and then a gasp.

It's so intense, this pleasure, I find myself straining away from it. Not because it doesn't feel divine, but because the human body cannot have been made to withstand this kind of sensual torture.

"Oh, no, you don't," he blows the words over one damp, tight nipple when I squirm. "Stay put."

"August." My back arches when his lips wander between my breasts and track a line down the center of my stomach. He pauses at my belly, still flat, no sign of life from the outside view.

"Our baby's here, Iris," August says, his voice thickening with emotion. He glances up, his lips pressed to the sensitive skin covering my pubic bone. "How did that even happen?"

"How did it happen?" I spread my legs, rubbing my thigh against the smooth naked musculature of his back. "Should I refresh your memory on how we made a baby, Mr. West?"

His smile is strung together by lust and mischief.

"I think you should, Mrs. West." He kisses my hip and lingers over my abdomen. "You know I forget shit."

"Well, first there was a little of this." I lean up until our lips are a breath apart, slide my fingers into the decadence of his thick curls, and tug until our mouths meet. We moan into the kiss, and he adjusts to rest on his elbows and takes my face between his hands, devouring me. His tongue is on an adventure, seeking out all my wild, untamed places. I answer with growls and bites and feral sounds as our tongues wrestle, wrangle. I lose the thread of time; lose myself in the kiss until the insistent throb between my legs reminds me of what I need.

"Now," I say, breath labored like I've been running. "It takes more than a kiss to make a baby."

"I've heard that," August says, panting into the skin of my neck. "Tell me more."

"Well there may have been a little of this, too." I slide my naked body down the bed, his body a bridge of muscle and bone and taut, honeyed skin suspended over me. All along the way, I feather kisses over his nipples and the ridges of his abs, relishing his harshly-drawn breaths and the way his body clenches at my touch. When I reach his hips, I have no time for flirting and banter. I grip his ass, one cheek in each hand, and take his dick in my mouth. At this angle, with him over me, it's like stuffing him down my throat. He's in a position of power, and as soon as my lips close around him, he asserts that power. He leverages himself on one arm, on his elbow, but reaches with the other to tangle his fingers in my hair, angling my head so my mouth opens wider, takes more of him before I even ask for it. He pumps aggressively, like my mouth is my pussy. Like we're having sex. All that power, all that dick, in and out with force down my throat. At first I'm not sure I can take it for more than a few seconds, but something unlocks inside me after the initial aggressive thrusts, and I want more.

I drop my jaw and open my throat until his balls are at my chin. I toggle them in my hands, my grip firm and sure. I want to undo him, the same way he undoes me every time we make love.

"Fuck, Iris," he breathes heavily above me. "I can't . . . shit."

I slide my finger between the firm curves of his ass, insinuating my finger there. He goes still for a second, and I take advantage of his uncertainty, rubbing the puckered hole of his ass while swallowing every inch of my husband's dick. I let him go with a pop and take his balls, one at a time, into my mouth, lavishing each one with my tongue and lips.

"Oh, my God," he says over and over. "Iris, I'm gonna . . ."

I know he's close, and I need him too badly to be completely self-less and let him come anywhere except inside me. There's a fire traveling along my legs. I long to feel him stretching me. I release him from my mouth and turn onto my stomach. With the same stealth I slid down his body, I slide back up, until my back is pressed into his chest and my hips are aligned with him.

"I, uh, take it you want it from the back," he laughs, chest heaving.

"Hard, please."

He does not disappoint.

The first thrust pushes me up the bed, and I bury my face in a nearby pillow, angling my ass up for deeper penetration and also muffling the screams I know are forthcoming. We're sweating and grunting and it's so barbaric and beautiful, tears sting my eyes. My husband. My child growing inside of me. Our daughter in the room beside us. It's too much. I've come too far. I'm too grateful, and even as his last thrust comes so hard I might happily split right open, the dam holding back my tears, breaks. I come and convulse and weep, all of it a culmination of the night and our entire journey.

"God, August," I cry into the pillow. "I love you. Baby, I love you so much."

One strong arm circles around my midriff to pull my back tighter to his chest. Once we're both empty, done, he stands us on our knees. He's still inside me, and I wish he never had to leave. He scatters kisses over my neck and shoulders.

"Thank you," he mumbles. "For our baby, for Sarai, for loving me."

His voice breaks, and I realize the dampness I feel is not our sweat, but his tears. He buries his head in my hair, dropping kisses in the thick tresses at my neck.

"You're my world, Iris." I hear him swallow deeply, gulping down the emotion to get the words out. "Do you really know it? That you're the center of my whole world?"

He spreads his fingers over my belly, sniffs and kisses my ear. I link the fingers of one hand with his at my stomach and slide the other hand back and up into his hair and go limp against his chest.

"And you, August West," I whisper, not bothering to wipe away my own tears. "Are the center of mine."

Block Shot Stocking Stuffer

You must read BLOCK SHOT to appreciate this Christmas-themed
bonus material.
The events take place after the book.

Get BLOCK SHOT here: *https://amzn.to/2Pqu7OZ*

If you've read it,
did you miss Banner and Jared's TWO bonus chapters at the end of
their book?
You should read that before this bonus material!!!

Grab Their BONUS EPILOGUE
Click this link to receive the BONUS Epilogue
http://bit.ly/BlockBonusScene

Banner

"I'LL BE HOME FOR DINNER."

For most newly-married couples, that's probably a pretty standard thing to say, but for Jared and me, desperately trying to keep pace with the explosive growth of Elevation, our sports agency, these days it's rare.

"So will I," Jared replies, a smile breaking through the fatigue I detect even over the phone. "I have that meeting with Adidas, but I should be home by eight."

"So a *late* dinner." I signal the server for more water and search the crowded restaurant for my lunch companions. "That should give me time to cook."

"Or I could bring something home so you won't *have* to cook. You have a long day, too."

"Awwww. So thoughtful." I chuckle and smile my thanks to the server for the second glass of water he sets on the table. "But I want to cook. It'll help me unwind."

"There are better ways to unwind," Jared says, his voice humored and husky.

"Oh, we can do that, too, Foster. I *am* ovulating."

"*Ovulating*. So sexy. You know how all this reproductive foreplay turns me on."

"Shut it." My laughter comes quickly and fades just as fast. "I'm hoping this new prescription helps."

There's a brief silence filling up with Jared's concern.

"It hasn't been that long, Ban," he finally says softly. "A few months. It'll happen when it's supposed to."

"Says the man who isn't even sure he wants kids."

I regret the comment as soon as it leaves my mouth.

"Jared, I didn't mean—"

"I'm in, Banner," Jared replies, his gentleness turning firm. "You know that. Just because I'm not obsessed with having kids doesn't mean I don't want to. With *you* I want to."

I sigh, frustrated with myself, with my body, with whatever is keeping me from conceiving.

"I *do* know that. I'm sorry. I'm feeling edgy, anxious. And you're right. It hasn't been long, but I hear that huge clock ticking."

"Forget the damn imaginary clock."

"It's not imaginary, Jared. The doctor said my estrogen levels are low. She thinks I may be at risk for early menopause. Coupled with my PCOS, it just feels like this needs to happen now. She all but *said* this needs to happen now."

"We'll have our kids when the time is right. I don't care if I have to hang you upside down and impregnate you with a turkey baster."

"Ew."

"Or if it's IVF," he goes on, ignoring my mild disgust. "Or adoption."

"Don't give up on me yet." I swallow the sudden lump in my throat. "Don't give up on us having kids the old-fashioned way yet. We're just getting started."

"My point exactly," Jared slices in. "We just started trying to get pregnant, and I for one, plan to enjoy all the trying, Mrs. Morales-Foster."

His comment coaxes an involuntary smile from me. How many times has he talked me out of discouragement? Raised my spirits with his dark humor and made me laugh when I thought it wasn't possible.

"Still rankles, does it?" I tease. "The hyphen?"

His answering chuckle assures me it does not.

"No, because hyphen or no hyphen, your pussy is still mine."

"Jared." I swallow a giggle, glancing around the restaurant as if he's on speaker phone and everyone can hear. "You're incorrigible."

"When you talk smart, my dick gets hard."

"Obviously this conversation is deteriorating." I shake my head, a grin taking my lips hostage. "And I have a meeting."

"Give Zo my best," Jared says easily. The tension that used to suffuse our conversations about my ex-boyfriend and still-client isn't there.

"And Graciella," I add. "She's coming, too."

"Even better. Are they still going to the orphanage for Christmas?"

"Yeah, leaving for Argentina tomorrow."

Zo's tall figure fills the doorway, and he searches the dining room. A smile lights his face when he spots me.

"They're here," I tell Jared, even though right now I only see Zo.

"Okay, I'll see you at home for dinner. I love you."

"So much," I reply, having to swallow that stupid lump in my throat again. "Thank you, Jared, for the perspective, the support, the—"

"You can thank me after dinner. I gladly accept sexual favors."

"Goodbye, Mr. Foster."

"Later, Mrs. Morales-Foster."

As soon as we hang up, I stand and step into the warm hug Zo has waiting for me.

"Hola, Bannini," he says, dropping a kiss into my hair. "Estas preciosa."

"Gracias." I pull back and grin up at him, affection for my old friend warming my smile as I continue in Spanish. "You don't look too bad yourself. You're the picture of health."

He nods, but his smile slips a bit.

"You are, right?" I demand and study his handsome face more closely. "You're okay? What does your doctor say?"

"I'm as good as I can possibly be. They want to try a new drug. Experimental. They say because of my excellent conditioning, I'm a perfect candidate for it, but I'm not sure I want to tempt fate by changing a thing."

I sit and gesture for him to take one of the other seats at the table.

"What are the risks?" I ask, a frown tugging my brows together. "Is there any empirical evidence? Has it worked for anyone else? Why would you—"

"Banner," he cuts in softly, a faint warning there.

A wry grin tips my mouth. It's none of my concern anymore. He's right, and keeping my nose out of his business, other than his *actual* business, is what keeps things comfortable for both of our significant others. Hell, for us, too.

"Sorry." I fiddle with the linen napkin on the table. "Old habits die hard."

"You know I'll never forget all you did for me." Zo covers my hand with his briefly before pulling back. "I wouldn't even be alive if it weren't for you."

"You're exaggerating." I dip my head to hide the emotion that nearly overwhelms me when I think about all the times he came within a handbreadth of dying.

"No, I'm not," Zo replies. "And we both know. Only we really know, Banner."

I lift my head to find a matching emotion reflected in his eyes. We've been through a lot together. Hell together, actually, but now we're both happier than we've ever been.

"Where's Graciela?" I ask, reaching for my water to take a sip. "I thought she was coming with you."

"Yes, she, uh . . ." Zo twists his lips, something close to discomfort flitting across his expression. "She needed the restroom. There's something I need to tell you, Bannini, before we dive into my speaking schedule for next year."

I grab the iPad from its slot in my leather bag.

"What's up?" I place the iPad on the table, sit back and cross my legs, waiting for him to continue.

"Gracie and I, we're engaged."

I cover my immediate smile with one hand, joy popping off inside me like champagne corks. I may even squeal.

"Dios, Zo, that's fantastic." I lean forward to capture and hold his gaze with mine, letting him see how sincerely delighted I am for him. "You deserve every happiness."

"Gracias," Zo answers, his proud grin widening. "She has no idea what she's getting into, so I'll marry her before she figures out she's getting a lemon."

"Lemon, my ass. You're in better shape than most of those guys playing in the league. Still."

"Yeah, well, there's something else I need to tell you." That shadow passes over his face again. "Banner, Gracie is—"

"Sorry about that," Graciela's voice interrupts as she reaches the table. "I hear lots of bathroom breaks are to be expected for women in my condition."

I glance up, and my smile freezes.

Pregnant.

That's the word Zo didn't get to say. The thing he was uncomfortable telling me. He knows how badly I want a baby; knows we've been trying with no success so far.

I flick a glance from the little bump poking through Graciela's loose-fitting dress to her pretty face.

"Yes, I hear that, too," I reply on auto-pilot. "Congratulations on both counts."

"Gracias," she says, her expression turning dreamy when she places a delicate hand on her belly.

Her engagement ring catches the sun streaming through the wall of windows, and a shard of light pokes my eye. Makes me squint. It cuts like glass across my face, and for a moment, pain slices through me. It has nothing to do with the ring, and everything to do with the baby growing inside Zo's fiancée.

"How far along are you?" I ask, relying on muscle memory for my smile as she takes her seat.

"Five months." Graciela meets my smile and turns one to Zo, but Zo is looking at me.

"I was going to tell you, Banner," he says quickly.

He knows. I hate that I can't hide from either of the men who have meant so much to me, Zo as a friend and Jared as the love of my life. In this moment, with LA's blinding winter sun exposing every emotion in me, on my face, there is nowhere to hide.

"Oh, no," I rush to assure him . . . and her. "Why? Most couples get past the first trimester before telling people."

But I'm not "people" and it is well into the second trimester, and even if Graciela doesn't know, Zo and I both know why he didn't tell me.

"We haven't spoken as much lately either," Zo continues, a defensive note creeping into his voice.

It's true. Since he retired, he has withdrawn from the public eye as he shored up his health in preparation for next year's aggressive schedule.

"I know," I say, a more natural smile melting away the fake one. "And I'm glad I haven't had to bother you. It sounds like your medical team is on top of making sure you're ready for next year."

Zo searches my face, looking for clues to how I'm really feeling.

Leave it alone, Zo.

After the initial shock of hearing about Graciela's pregnancy, I'm settling into what should have been my first response. Happiness for him.

"It's amazing," I tell Graciela, but for Zo's benefit. I pick up the menu and find the salad I have enough points for. "Mama will be delighted. She was so concerned about this when you were in treatment.

I'm glad you prepared for this."

"And we didn't even have to use the sperm he set aside," Graciela says with a chuckle. "We weren't even trying. Can you believe that?"

"I can't believe it," I murmur through numb lips. "That's amazing."

I'm not sure how many times I can say "amazing" before it starts sounding insincere. And I *do* mean it. I *am* happy for them. I'm just not happy for me. Zo, who's sperm the doctors said would probably never produce children, wasn't even trying and has a baby on the way. I'm doing everything short of a virgin sacrifice, and nothing.

I'm able to set aside my selfish peevishness and get through lunch. Over a delicious meal, we discuss their plans for Christmas at the orphanage and, more extensively, the book Zo has been writing and the travel schedule I've started organizing for next year.

"So after the holidays," I say, pushing aside the remnants of my salad. "We go to New York and meet with publishers. I have ten lined up ready to hear our pitch, but we're really the ones considering *them*. Everyone will want your story, Zo."

"If I can stay healthy long enough to tell it." Zo says it lightly, but I know him well enough to hear the real fear in his voice. I was there when the doctor diagnosed him with amyloidosis. It was a death sentence, one he'll be outrunning the rest of his life. It's easy for me to say he'll be fine; that he should take risks and experiment, but he's the one who has flatlined and been brought back. He's the one who lived through chemo and the debilitation of stem cell replacement. Him sitting at this table is a miracle.

His baby is a miracle.

"I need to use the bathroom one more time before we go," Graciela says, her dark eyes meeting Zo's in a private contentment only they can share. "The story of my life lately. I'll be right back."

I snatch the bill off the table before Zo can grab it.

"I'm expensing it," I say, stuffing my card in the leather sleeve and handing it to the server. "So back off my bill."

He shakes his head and smiles, but concern quickly replaces the humor in his eyes.

"I was going to tell you, Bannini," he says softly.

"Please." I hold up a hand to stop whatever he's about to say. "Don't feel bad at all. It's your news to share as you see fit. *When* you see fit. It's fine."

"No one was more shocked than me. When Gracie turned up pregnant, I couldn't believe it at first."

"If anyone deserves a miracle, it's you, Zo."

"It'll happen for you, too."

I can't bear the sympathy in his eyes one more second. As soon as the server returns with my card, I sign and stand.

"I need to get back to the office," I say abruptly.

He stands, too, immediately dwarfing me. I punch one well-muscled bicep.

"Welcome to the gun show," I tease. "You sure you're done with ball? Looks like you could still hold your own out there."

"Looks can be deceiving." He loops an arm around my neck and pulls me close. "He still treating you right, Bannini?"

He's only half-joking. He's as concerned about my happiness as I am for his.

"Jared treats me like a queen." I pull back enough to smile up at him. "He's the best thing that's ever happened to me."

"He's one lucky son of a bitch, is what he is." A smile crinkles Zo's eyes at the corners. "But he knows that."

"Yes, he knows that."

I disentangle myself and grab the bag I almost left in my haste to get the heck out.

"Tell Graciela I had to dash." I turn to go.

"Love you, Banner," Zo says softly.

I stop and look over my shoulder, catching the deep affection he holds for me in the glance we share. How many people are lucky enough to have friendships like this? Enduring friendships tried by fire that have survived the worst circumstances? Friends who have forgiven and forgotten transgressions so they don't lose one another.

"Love you, too, Zo."

I make my way out of the restaurant, guiltily hoping I don't run into Graciela and her adorable baby bump again. When I do actually get pregnant, I don't think it'll be cute. Some women just have that delicate adorableness and subtle glow during pregnancy. I fully anticipate sweating like a stuck pig and blowing up to the size of Cleveland, judging by the pregnancies of my mother, aunts and every childbearing woman in my family to date.

Of necessity, I've learned to compartmentalize. This business, this pace, doesn't slow down for anyone. Definitely not for a woman leading one of the fastest-growing sports agencies around. There's no time for the disappointment settling in layers of sediment at the bottom of my belly. No time for the anxiety that would paralyze me if I stop moving. No time for the senseless envy blurring my vision as I think about that little mound under Graciela's dress. There's no room for jealousy. I have no right to it, so I set each and every blistering emotion aside and get back to work.

I soldier through meetings and conference calls, but in the back of my mind, I'm longing for this one spot, for this one moment as soon as the day is over. I think about that spot on the ride home. When I walk through the door, I pause in the foyer to absorb the quiet. After talking all day, pitching and persuading and negotiating, the silence is a relief. I need a little space to sort through all I've felt; how vulnerable and emotional I've been.

I strip away my suit and heels, carelessly discarding them on the closet floor. I've been caged by the silk sleeves sheathing my arms and the belt cinching my waist; corseted by the underwear disciplining my body into smoother lines and slimmer curves. The bra, the body shaper—gone, and it feels like my whole being releases a deep breath it's been holding since I dressed this morning. I pad over to Jared's side of the closet and rummage in his drawers until I find an old Kerrington College t-shirt. I wander up the hall to a room I haven't allowed myself to think about much lately, but thought about all the way home.

Right now this guest bedroom only holds a few of Jared's things from his old apartment; refugee furniture, displaced and finding no natural spot in this house, several boxes of books, and his Play Station, which I've basically outlawed. Grown men screaming on headsets and pretending to blow things up, that's not advancing humanity in any way. He's complied, but insists I keep him entertained sexually if he can't play his games.

Fair trade.

This room is otherwise empty. Barren. Like me.

But when the realtor first showed this house, I was drawn to the window seat in here; how the soon-setting sun shone through glass and brightened the entire room. I envisioned myself sitting here feeding my baby and singing one of the *arrullos* my mama sang to my sister Camilla and me.

The last of the day's light beckons me to the bench where my kindle lies abandoned on the cushion, dead and dusty. A few weeks ago I slipped in here to catch up on some reading, but Jared strode in growling something about less reading, more fucking. The rest is a blur.

The lyrics of "A La Nanita" tickle my memory, and a soft hum vibrates in my throat. A carol and lullaby to the baby Jesus, we'd sing it especially at Christmas, but I heard it crooned to babies in every season throughout my life.

A la nanita nana
nanita ella, nanita ella
Mi niñ(a) tiene sueño
bendito sea, bendito sea
Fuentecita que corre
Clara y sonora
Ruiseñor que en la selva

Cantando y llora
Calla mientras la cuna
Se balancea
A la nanita nana
Nanita ella

My favorite line is *My little girl is sleepy, blessed is she, blessed is she.*

Am I blessed? I know the answer is a resounding yes. I have more than most. I'm fed and clothed and safe with, not just a roof over my head, but an expensive roof that no one in my family ever believed we'd have. I'm married to the only man I've ever really loved, and he loves me back to near obsession.

And yet I sit here, stewing in self-pity and envy, feeling cursed. I'm struck again with the irony of Graciela and Zo, pregnant against every odd without even trying, and me consumed by the thought of having a baby and . . . nothing. Is this punishment for my sins? For cheating on Zo? Aunt Valentina would say yes. She'd hand me one of her rosaries and send me to confession, but even though I've been raised a good Catholic girl, that doesn't feel right. "A La Nanita" was originally penned as a lullaby for Jesus. Surely there is grace? Forgiveness? I know it was wrong, what I did, but will I be punished? Is this punishment? Or is this just life? Indiscriminate destiny blindly serving up good and bad.

Even as the thoughts flit through my mind like acrid smoke, I know they're not true. I'm not being punished. *Truth* is I have Polycystic Ovary Syndrome. PCOS makes it harder for me to get pregnant. *Fact* is that we haven't even been trying that long. Truth and fact war with a desire I've held for as long as I can remember. I've always wanted to be a mother; to instill in my little girls the confidence it took me too long to find. To raise sweet little boys into powerful, respectful men. I have to believe those weren't doomed dreams, but there is hope. Right now, I just can't find it. I can't feel it.

"Ban!"

Jared yells my name from the foyer entry. I open my mouth to answer, but tears clog my throat. I've been a ball of emotions all day, tearing up over nothing. I need to get my shit together if I don't want a lecture from Jared.

And I don't want a lecture from Jared.

"Banner," Jared calls again, his voice accompanied by approaching steps. He's checking our bedroom, but of course I'm not there.

"In here," I manage, mopping the tears wetting my cheeks. My husband's eyes are as sharp as his mind. I've been on the defending side of both more than once, and would rather not explain a sting he'll only want to soothe. Sometimes you don't want to be soothed. Sometimes you want to ache. You want to feel the pain because it's attached to something so vital, so important, it's worth the hurt because it will make the ultimate joy that much richer. I just wonder if joy is in store for me.

"Did I screw up?" Jared asks from the doorway, dark blond eyebrows pinched over weary blue eyes. "Was I supposed to grab dinner? I thought you said—"

"I did say." I sink deeper into the cushions, deeper into the shadows filling the room now that the sun has gone down. "I planned to cook, but came up here and got, um . . . I lost track of time, I guess."

He reaches toward the wall and flicks on the light. I squint against the sudden brightness, lowering my head so my hair covers my face. I'm reminded of our first kiss, of our first time making love in the dark. He wanted the light on, but I insisted we leave it off. I promised him and myself I was done hiding in the dark, but with the unreasonable ache in my heart on display and probably all over my face, I want to beg him to turn out the light. Jared narrows his eyes, the look he gives me sharpening. He crosses the room in a few strides to stand in front of me and tips up my chin.

"You've been crying. What's going on?"

I turn my head a few inches to loosen my chin from his fingers.

"I'm fine." I stand up and step around him. "Dinner will take no time."

He catches me by the elbow, his touch gentle and firm.

"To hell with dinner. What's wrong?"

I close my eyes against the bright overhead light and against his probing stare. He's concerned. It's mixing in his eyes with love and stubbornness, a recipe for Jared's tenacity. I've tasted it firsthand for years. When the man wants something, he doesn't let up until he has it. That was true with his dreams, his goals.

His wife.

Usually, I'm here for it. Ready to match him, toe to toe, but tonight, there's no fight, especially when the thing he's fighting for is me.

"Graciela's pregnant," I say softly, dropping my glance to the floor.

"Oh." Jared lets me go and crosses his arms over his chest. "Congratulations to them."

"They're also engaged, by the way."

"Even better for them. We can send a plant or whatever you send when people procreate. What does that have to do with you sitting in a dark room crying and losing track of time, which is bullshit, by the way, because you don't lose track of time?"

"Don't." I run a hand through the hair tangled around my shoulders. "Please don't tough love me right now. I can't take it."

"Then how should I love you?" He cups my face, tilting my head until our eyes meet. "Tell me what you think you need, and I'll see if I agree."

A humorless smile tips one corner of my mouth. He's a bulldozer, but tonight I'm already flat.

"They weren't even trying, Jared," I whisper. "It just happened for them. For her, and the doctor said it was so unlikely. But, boom. He breathes on her and she's having a baby. They didn't even have to use the sperm Zo set aside before he started his treatments."

"First of all, that's a lot more than I wanted to *ever* know about Zo's reproductive capabilities."

My lips twitch, but I refuse to laugh. "Do not try to cheer me up."

"I don't want to cheer you up. I want to *wake* you up."

"Thank you, Tony Robbins." I roll my eyes and start for the door.

He takes my elbow again, tugging until I'm standing in front of him.

"Hey." He pushes a swathe of hair behind my ear and lifts my face. "You're stronger than this."

"Am I?" I shake my head and a runaway tear skids over my cheek. "What if my PCOS ruins everything? What if the doctor is right, and I get early onset menopause? What if—"

"Yeah, what if all of that is true? What if it happens?" He waves his hand, motioning for me to continue. "What else you got?"

I'm quiet, hurting.

"Oh?" He cocks his head. "You're out already? I've got some. What if I'm sterile? What if you're in a wreck and your ovaries are crushed? What if my dick falls off from overuse?"

"Okay." I snort involuntarily as he knew I would. "That's not a thing."

"Lucky for you," he says, relenting a small smile before going on. "My point is there's no scenario you can dream up where I don't love you, Banner. None of those things mean I don't have you for the rest of our lives."

I look up, captured by the passion in his voice, the earnestness on his face.

"I know you think I don't want kids, and honestly, I never did," he admits. "But I want to experience everything with you because everything is better with you. Life is better with you. I want to live it and not worry about what might happen, why it's not happening fast enough, why it's happening for someone else. All of it's happening with *you*, and that means we face everything together. We *have* everything together."

And we have so much.

I hate it when he's right, but he's so right. I've allowed this irrational fear and dissatisfaction to wreck my entire day. It road blocked my excitement for what is essentially Zo's miracle. It had me snapping at the man I love more than anything in the world. Is there a lobotomy for emotions because I could do without them today.

"You're right," I finally say.

"No surprise there."

I give him a quelling look to let him know he's pushing it.

"Sorry," he says, an unrepentant grin crooking his lips.

"Liar." I chuckle and reach up to link my wrists behind his neck. "I can count on one hand how many times you've been sorry since I met you."

It's not an insult or a reprimand. I don't need a man who apologizes for what he wants, for what he believes. Jared is a man of conviction. All completely his own, and I need that sometimes. That unshaken demeanor; his *I don't give a fuck* on days like today when everything feels like salt poured over an open wound.

"The way I look at it," Jared says, slipping wide palms up my bare thighs and under the t-shirt to grip my ass. "We could stand around talking about having a baby, or we could try to make one."

He ghosts kisses down my neck, sucking the curve to my shoulder

"Are we really gonna let all that super sexy ovulating go to waste, Banner?"

"We shouldn't."

I tunnel my fingers into the thick silkiness of his hair and walk us backward until he's sitting on the window seat and I'm straddling him. With one hand he reaches between my legs and pushes my panties aside. He brushes over my clit, my lips, through the wet folds until he reaches the hot, waiting center and thrusts two fingers inside me. Unceremoniously. He tips his head back to rest against the window and watches my face for the response I can't hide.

"Jared, dammit." I rock into his hand and press my forehead to his.

He pulls me down farther, widening my knees over him and pushing my Kindle out of the way. It lands with a quiet thud on the carpeted floor.

"You need to be gentler with my kindle," I tell him, my laugh breathless; my lips following a hungry path up to his earlobe.

"What'd I tell you?" His laugh is husky. His eyes, heated, loving. "Less reading. More fucking."

Jared

I know how I want to ring in the New Year, and it's not at this party schmoozing some dick who keeps looking down my wife's dress. I mean, I get it. Banner looks sexy as hell. Her strapless dress defies gravity, magically supporting the fullness of her breasts. The red silk hugs the dip at her waist, stretches over the flare of her hips and caresses the curve of her ass.

"Would you excuse us, Claude?" I ask, slicing into whatever nonsense he's spouting while rudely ogling Banner at my side. "There's someone over there we need to see."

I gesture vaguely across the room. Claude, president of one of the largest sports drink companies in North America, turns his head in that general direction. By the time he looks back, I'm already leading Banner away.

"See you at the All-Star break," I call, glancing back to give him a NutraSweet smile. "You'll be there, right?"

He opens his mouth to answer, but I don't give a shit, and am tired of pretending I do.

"Great," I answer before he can respond. "Happy New Year. Give your wife our best."

"I don't think he's married," Banner murmurs, smiling at a Gatorade executive with whom she's been hammering out a deal for one of our clients.

"Oh, that explains why he couldn't keep his eyes off *my* wife," I answer from one side of my mouth and grinning at a VP of basketball operations with the other. "I'm ready to get the hell outta here."

She stops in the middle of the room, which makes me stop, too.

"Jared, you were the one who wanted to do this industry party on New Year's Eve." Her eyes go wide, long lashes feathering up to the thick arch of her eyebrows.

"Don't even try it." I laugh down at her, my hand tightening at her waist because it's so hard not kissing her in front of all these people right the fuck now. "You said there would be contacts here we needed for the next few months."

"Okay, maybe I did say that." She bites her bottom lip, which makes me envy her teeth because I want to bite her bottom lip just like that.

No harder.

"But *I* said let's just stop through," she continues, a grin crinkling her eyes at the corners. "*You* were the one who got us roped into that long conversation on unrestricted free agency."

"We need to know that guy." I take her elbow and set us in motion again. "He's working with the NBA Player's Union."

"Did you forget that Kenan's on the executive committee of the Player's Union?"

"Oh, yeah." I shrug, but don't stop our forward momentum. I have a goal in mind. "Not a waste of time, I promise you."

I wave to a retired player who has been requesting a meeting with us for representation. Not tonight, dude.

"Where are we going?" Banner asks. She glances over her shoulder and then forward down the long corridor ahead of us. The music and murmur of conversation and tinkling liquor-filled glasses fades the farther we venture down the darkened hall. "Are we supposed to be down here?"

"Our host has this incredible library with a view of the hills." I look back over my shoulder to make sure no one is following us. All clear. "It's right in here."

I open the door to our right and give Banner a gentle shove inside. She stumbles a little and swings around to face me, the dark length of her hair arcing out behind her.

"What the hell?" she asks, her mouth slightly open and her expression startled.

I don't leave her time to wonder, but lock the door and pin her to the shelf of books against the wall.

"All night," I mutter against the satiny column of her neck. "I have been wanting you all night."

"Jared." She laughs, a flush sifting pink into her honey gold complexion. "We're gonna get caught. Stop playing."

"Does this feel like I'm playing?" I press my erection into the cradle of her hips. "I'm as serious as a heart attack. Or maybe a hard on. I'm as serious as a hard on."

"You . . . we can't." She looks up at me, and I hear what she's saying, but I know that look. It's the sense of adventure my girl leashes when she's not sure she should take a risk. And I'm the guy who sets that leash on fire. I tug at the neckline of her strapless dress, and her breasts fall free. I squat and take one nipple in my mouth, groaning and slipping my hand under her dress and up her thigh.

"Jared." She pants and wrings my hair in her fingers tightly. "That feels . . . you're really gonna do this here?"

"Yes, here." I push her panties aside, thrusting my middle finger into the warm, wet tunnel of her pussy. "These are such a waste of time. I wish you'd stop wearing them."

"Panties?" She breathes a laugh. "You want me to stop wearing panties?"

"They slow me down." I dip my head to kiss her, tangling our tongues and licking across her teeth. "God, I could just eat you. Fuck, Ban. You're so good."

She thinks I'm exaggerating about how I want her; how I need her. She thinks I like to have sex in public to be outrageous, but most of the time I simply can't resist her. I don't want to. I don't want to wait until we get home, or until it's safe. Why the hell should I? I found someone I could love, no holds barred. I luxuriate in that. I want her every chance I get, and safe doesn't mean shit to me.

"I love you. You're everything." I mumble between our lips, into the kiss. "Fuck safe."

"I love you back." She breaks the kiss to look into my eyes, but leaves our bodies molded together. "Fuck safe."

She turns quickly to face the shelves, pressing her naked breasts into a row of books.

"From the back," she says, her voice urgent. Her hands frantic and pushing the dress up over her thighs, over her ass. The thong bisects two perfectly round globes of my wife's ass, and I almost come immediately like a fourteen-year-old getting his first nut. I fumble with my belt and snag my finger in the teeth of the zipper.

"Ouch. Shit." I suck my finger and drop my pants, angling her hips for me.

"Unf." The sound flies from her mouth when I take her from behind, pounding up and into her. "Yes. God, yes, Jared. *Dios. Dios. Dios.*"

I don't have the heart to remind her to be quiet. With every thrust, her screams swell louder, and it's the most arousing sound I've ever heard. I love peeling back all Banner's carefully constructed layers of control and freeing the wild woman who blindly reaches behind until she finds my bare ass and urges me deeper and harder.

I squeeze one breast and push the length of wavy hair away from her neck. The skin, smooth and unblemished, has tempted me all night. When the passion cools, if she has to walk out there with a hickey for a roomful of our colleagues to see, she'll kill me. But I have to leave my mark; to lay my claim, even if it is a secret nestled under a thick fall of hair that no one else sees. I suck and bite the soft skin of her nape, steadily pumping into her body with unchecked force, yielding to the feral urges that have seized me by the dick ever since she came out of our bedroom wearing this dress. I lick at the bruise already forming, and her pussy contracts around me; a hot, wet, tight fist that holds me captive.

God, I'm gonna come.

And she hasn't come.

I hate that. I've never felt that with another woman. I mean, as a point of pride, you want a woman to get off, yeah. But with Banner, it's not pride. I literally want her pleasure above mine. Considering what a selfish bastard I am, that's a phenomenon. A miracle like one of Aunt Valentina's pieces of toast that looks just like Baby Jesus.

I reach around and find the button of nerves tucked between the plump lips and stroke.

"Ay, Dios mío," she mutters, slamming her fist into the shelf she's pressed against. "Más fuerte."

Harder.

I can do that. I push up into her so hard, I glance down to see her on her tiptoes. Damn right.

"Más," Banner growls, squeezing my butt. "Fuerte".

Shit, my wife loves it hard.

"Ban, I don't want—"

"Por favor, lo necesito más fuerte."

How the hell any husband could resist his wife begging him to fuck her harder, I don't know. And I'm for sure not that guy, so I brace one palm against the shelf and grip her hip with the other hand and slam as far as I can go into nirvana pussy.

"Fuuuuuuuuuck," I whisper. I can barely speak, the pleasure is so thick. A tangible thing like a heavy cloud hovering over us, poised to downpour. A book falls, barely missing Banner's head.

"Ban, the books—"

"Cògeme.," she orders, her voice a smoky rasp.

Fuck me.

Dammit, if it's the last thing I do, I *will* fuck her harder, even if the whole damn Dewey Decimal system falls on our heads before we both come.

I exert more force and sweat beads my forehead. Peering over her shoulder, I see tiny rivulets of perspiration slide between Banner's breasts. Three more books drop by my feet.

"Ahhhhhh!" The scream is wrenched from her throat, and she tips her head back to rest on my shoulder. "Shit, Jared. Yes."

A shudder runs through her soft curves, and she contracts around me, squeezing every ounce of pleasure out of the connection between our bodies.

Okay. We definitely have a walk of shame when we leave this library, but I don't give a damn because an orgasm takes ruthless possession of my entire body. Fire claws through my blood, smoke blows over the nerve endings in my calves, thighs. A tremor overtakes me as I empty into my woman.

"Fuck. Fuck. Fuck." Every word is accompanied by a piston thrust into my wife's limp body. Her back rests against my chest, and she's just receiving me now, so blissed out I have to hold her up when my *own* legs feel like Jell-O and I'm not sure how much longer I can stand. An upper shelf rains down several books, and I have to shift us a few inches to avoid the falling hardbacks.

Banner's husky chuckle comes as I'm finishing inside her, coming down, crashing hard. I push her hair aside again, licking the hickey I left on the back of her neck and scattering kisses across her bare shoulders.

"¿De qué te ríes?" I ask. She loves it when I speak Spanish. It's not my native language like it is for her, and she's been helping me get better at it.

"I'm laughing at us wrecking this poor man's library," she replies in Spanish.

At least I *think* that's what she says.

"We'll clean up." I glance from the books to the upper shelves from which they fell. "Well what we can reach."

I lean deeper into her back for a moment, relishing the dampness of her skin. I kiss the hair curling at her neck from perspiration.

My hands go to her hips and then around to cup her stomach where the bodice of her dress bunches at her waist. The original reason I suggested the party rushes back to mind. August and Iris called from San Diego with good news. They're having a baby. Is the whole damn world fertile? I'm pelted with pregnant women at every turn.

Banner didn't flinch or wince or even grimace at the news, but gave them the full measure of her enthusiasm. We laughed with them and even talked about it after they hung up. I asked Banner if she was fine, and she assured me she was. I even believed her.

Still.

I thought getting out of the house on New Year's Eve might be a good distraction if she felt any lingering disappointment that it's not our time yet.

"You sure you're okay?" I ask, rubbing my chin into her hair.

She covers my hands on her stomach with hers and leans back, tilting her head to catch the concern I know must be in my eyes.

"Jared, I told you I'm fine."

She smiles, and that dimple dents her cheek. My heart pinches. I knew in college there was something about this woman that would captivate me forever if I let it. If I let *her*. Turns out there was no *letting*. I had no choice in the matter. Even shoving it to the back of my mind for years did no good. As soon as I was in Banner's orbit again, I was hers. And she was mine, even though I had to take her from Zo.

Collateral damage.

God knows Zo has been through enough and deserves some good. Hearing that he and Graciela are having a baby, I'm happy for them. And I was happy for Gus and Iris. Of course, I am. I'm gonna be an uncle again. But I want to make sure my girl is processing it all well.

She pulls away, and I hate leaving her body. I spot a box of Kleenex on the edge of the desk and grab a handful.

"Hey." I pull her around to face me, and holding her gaze with mine, reach under her dress between her legs and wipe at the wetness leaking down the inside of her thighs before pulling her thong back in place. Her lashes flutter and she looks up at me, fresh desire in her eyes. She's as easily turned on as I am.

Hallelujah.

"When we get home," I say, leaning to toss the Kleenex in the trash before pulling her dress up to cover those glorious breasts. "I'm fucking you again."

"You took the words right out of my mouth, Foster," she says, her laugh low and naughty.

"You just worry about what I'm putting *in* your mouth before the night is over."

"Blowing in the New Year." She smiles and licks her lips. "I like it."

We're sliding the last fallen books back in place when, through the library window, a few preliminary fireworks flash like a fire-flung kaleidoscope over the iconic Hollywood hills. Seconds later the countdown begins, faint and drifting from the party down the hall.

Ten. Nine.

"It's almost midnight," Banner says, anticipation widening her smile.

Eight. Seven.

"Yup." I turn her back into the shelf and cage her with my elbows on either side of her shoulders. "Trapping you in here was part of my evil plan to kiss you at midnight with no one watching."

Six. Five.

She laughs, eyes bright and a flush of excitement on her cheeks.

"Well, it worked," she says.

Four. Three.

I cup her face and lower my head, savoring the last few seconds of the year we're leaving behind and the one that's ahead with the only woman I adore.

"Jared, I have something to tell you," she whispers over my lips.

Two.

"I'm pregnant."

One.

She tips up and takes my mouth with hers, kissing me deeply as her words penetrate my consciousness. On instinct, I kiss her back, loving the feel of her, the intimacy of her touch, even while my lips go numb with the shock of what I *think* she said.

I force myself to break our kiss.

"Ban, what'd you say? I thought you said you're—"

"Pregnant," she repeats softly, a wide smile stretching the same-size lips I've never been able to resist. "You know my period is kind of sporadic because of the PCOS, so my cycle isn't my best gauge, but I was a little late and decided to take the test. I was bracing myself to be disappointed, but I wasn't. I'm pregnant."

She actually giggles. My Banner, who never giggles, is giddy.

"Maybe that's why I've been so emotional," she goes on, the words tripping from her lips in a rush. "I hope it passes. I can't go through nine months like that."

Shock paralyzes me for a full five seconds before something else floods every cell of my body. I have no idea what to name this emotion. I've never felt anything like it. It's akin to the love I have for Banner, but doubled, tripled, multiplied. Exponential.

"Are you . . ." Her smile dims. Her arms drop from my neck and she swallows, her eyes never leaving my face. "You're not . . . are you not happy?"

She slides along the shelf and away from me, and the rush of cool air her absence brings jolts me out of this mute state of idiocy.

"God, yes, Ban." I snatch her back and wrap my arms all the way around her and lift until her feet leave the floor.

"Jared!" she screeches. "Put me down. I'm too heavy."

"No, you're not." I shift my arms under her ass, and she rests her elbows on my shoulders, presses her forehead to mine. "I'm gonna be better, Ban. I promise."

"What?" She draws back just enough to glance down at me.

"Better than what?"

"A better man." I swallow the knot of emotion burning my throat. "I can be better. For our baby, I'll try to . . ."

Shit, I don't even know where to start. My dad was an amazing father. And August fell right into raising Sarai like it was a bike he'd ridden a thousand times, and he was just climbing back on. He'll be perfect for the second baby, too. And Zo's kid hit the lottery having a patron saint for a father. But my poor kid? Who the hell all knows what I'll do? How I'll screw it up.

Banner slides down my body until she's back on her feet. She reaches up, taking my face between her hands and forcing my eyes to meet hers.

"There's no one else I want to do this with, Foster," she says, eyes glassed with tears. "Our little girl is gonna be so badass."

A chuckle rumbles in my chest at her words, even though I'm still not sure I can do this shit.

"And our little boy will—"

"Wait," I cut in, my heart slamming into my ribs. "A girl *and* a boy? Are there like . . . two of them?"

Banner's laugh bounces off the library walls, and her body shakes against mine.

"You're an idiot." She smiles up at me and shakes her head. "I have no idea if there's one, two, three—'"

"Shit, Ban." I draw a deep breath and exhale heavily. "Just stop with multiples. I'm still wrapping my head around one."

"But you're happy?" Hesitation reins the excitement in her eyes. "I mean about the baby?"

I'm screwing this up already. I'm one scared son of a bitch. I have no idea if I can do this. Parents *nurture*. The closest I've ever come to nurturing anything is building a baller's career. I don't coddle or hand-hold.

But I'm honest. Ruthless, yes, but honest with it.

And I do believe in hard work.

And I know I have the capacity to love because I love Banner and my family, my closest friends.

Those seem like things I could pass on; things I could instill in a kid. Maybe I could start there.

"Happy doesn't even begin to describe it," I finally answer. "You're the only woman crazy enough to marry me, and I guess you're the only one crazy enough to let me father her kid."

We laugh together for a second, but looking at her, seeing the fireworks splash color through the library window across her face, I'm humbled to have another year with her. A new year. A new chapter of life with a woman I never thought I'd deserve.

"I love you, Ban." I shift my hands from her hips to the plane of her stomach. "And I already love our baby."

My words chase all hesitation from her eyes, from her expression, and that feeling that surged through me when she declared the news at the stroke of midnight, it's mirrored in the look she gives me. And I have a name for it now.

It's joy.

Curious about Iris & August?
Check out LONG SHOT here:
myBook.to/LongShotBook

If you would like to discuss BLOCK SHOT,
we have a place for that!
Join the discussion group here:
http://bit.ly/BSDiscuss

Listen to the music that inspired
Banner & Jared's journey
BLOCK SHOT Playlist:
http://bit.ly/BlockShotSpotify

Also by Kennedy Ryan

THE HOOPS SERIES
(3 Interconnected Standalone Stories)
FREE In KU!

LONG SHOT (A HOOPS Novel)
Available in Ebook, Audio & Paperback
https://amzn.to/2PrMrqQ

BLOCK SHOT (A HOOPS Novel)
Banner & Jared's Story

Enemies-to-Lovers | Friends-to-Lovers | Second Chance
https://amzn.to/2qtBhYo

Coming March 2019
HOOK SHOT (A HOOPS Novel)
Lotus & Kenan's Story
Add on Goodreads: http://bit.ly/KeLoGoodreads

Be alerted as SOON as it's LIVE:
Text KennedyRyan to 797979

Connect With Kennedy!

Never miss sales & new releases!

Follow me on Bookbub
www.bookbub.com/authors/kennedy-ryan

Text KennedyRyan to 797979 for new release alerts!

On Facebook, join my reader group for updates, fun and insider
scoop:
bit.ly/KennedyFBGroup

Like On Facebook:
facebook.com/KennedyRyanAuthor

Instagram:
instagram.com/kennedyryan1

Twitter:
twitter.com/kennedyrwrites

Newsletter:
bit.ly/KennedyMailingList

Follow on Amazon:
bit.ly/KennedyRyanBooks

Follow on Book + Main:
bookandmainbites.com/kennedyryan

ABOUT THE AUTHOR

A Top 30 Amazon Bestseller, Kennedy Ryan writes for women from all walks of life, empowering them and placing them firmly at the center of each story and in charge of their own destinies. Her heroes respect, cherish and lose their minds for the women who capture their hearts.

She is a wife to her lifetime lover and mother to an extraordinary son. She has always leveraged her journalism background to write for charity and non-profit organizations, but enjoys writing to raise Autism awareness most. A contributor for Modern Mom Magazine, Kennedy's writings have appeared in Chicken Soup for the Soul, USA Today and many others. The founder and executive director of a foundation serving Atlanta families living with Autism, she has appeared on Headline News, Montel Williams, NPR and other media outlets as an advocate for families living with autism.